The United St

Formed in 1789 by Presiden[...]
Marshals Service is the oldes[...]
in my mind, one of the mos[...]
death sentences, catch coun[...]
According to their Web site, "At virtually every significant point over
the years where Constitutional principles or the force of law have
been challenged, the marshals were there—and they prevailed." Now
the agency primarily focuses on fugitive investigation, prisoner/alien
transportation, prisoner management, court security and witness
security.

No big mystery there, you say? When I started this series, I didn't
think so, either. Intending to nail the details, I marched down to my
local marshals' office for an afternoon that will stay with me forever.

After learning the agency's history and being briefed on day-to-day
operations, I was taken on a tour. I saw an impressive courtroom
and a prisoner holding cell. Then we went to the garage to see
vehicles and bulletproof vests and guns. Sure, I'm an author, but I'm
primarily a mom and wife. I bake cookies and find hubby's always-
lost belt. Nothing made the U.S. Marshals Service spring to life for
me more than seeing those weapons. And then I realized my tour
guide wasn't fictional. He used those guns, put his very life on the
line protecting me and my family and the rest of this city, county
and state. I had chills.

Things really got interesting when I started digging for information
on the Witness Security Program. Deputy Marshal Rick ever so
politely sidestepped my every question. I found out nothing! Not
where the base of operations is located, not which marshals are
assigned to the program, what size crews are used, how their shifts
are rotated—nothing! After a while it got to be a game. One it was
obvious I'd lose!

Honestly, all this mystery probably makes for better fiction. I
don't want to know what really happens. It's probably not half as
romantic as the images of these great protectors I've conjured in my
mind. Oh—and another bonus to my tour—Deputy Marshal Rick
was Harlequin American Romance–hero hot!

Laura Altom

Dear Reader,

In case you couldn't already tell, I'm fascinated by the United States Marshals Service! Their Web site is wonderful, full of all sorts of interesting facts (www.usdoj.gov/marshals/index.html). Some of my favorite pages detail marshal-led sting operations. These guys are not only brave and strong, but funny!

One of the most elaborate stings involved free tickets to a Washington Redskins home football game against the Cincinnati Bengals. "The fugitives, wanted by authorities for a variety of criminal offenses, willingly gathered at the D.C. Convention Center in response to 'invitations' sent by the Marshals Service to the last known addresses of more than 3,000 wanted persons with more than 5,000 outstanding warrants." There are some super pics on the site, one of which features a pair of fugitives hamming it up with, unbeknownst to them, a U.S. Marshal dressed in a chicken suit!

Hoping any contests you win are the real deal,

Laura Marie

P.S. You can reach me through my Web site at www.lauramariealtom.com or write me at P.O. Box 2074, Tulsa, OK 74101.

His
Baby
Bonus

LAURA MARIE ALTOM

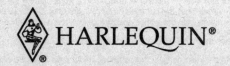

TORONTO • NEW YORK • LONDON
AMSTERDAM • PARIS • SYDNEY • HAMBURG
STOCKHOLM • ATHENS • TOKYO • MILAN • MADRID
PRAGUE • WARSAW • BUDAPEST • AUCKLAND

ISBN 0-373-75114-1

HIS BABY BONUS

This edition published by arrangement with Harlequin Books S.A.

® and TM are trademarks of the publisher. Trademarks indicated with
® are registered in the United States Patent and Trademark Office, the
Canadian Trade Marks Office and in other countries.

www.eHarlequin.com

Printed in U.S.A.

For United States Marshal Timothy D. Welch and
Deputy U.S. Marshal Rick Holden. Thank you for the
incredible tour of Tulsa's marshals' office, and for
patiently answering my gazillion questions!
Any technical errors are all mine!

And for sweet Edna Welch in the Nimitz Middle School
Library, who so tirelessly helps me find all those spy,
police and fairy-tale books.
Thank you for all your hugs and smiles!

Books by Laura Marie Altom

HARLEQUIN AMERICAN ROMANCE

Don't miss any of our special offers. Write to us at the
following address for information on our newest releases.

Harlequin Reader Service
U.S.: 3010 Walden Ave., P.O. Box 1325, Buffalo, NY 14269
Canadian: P.O. Box 609, Fort Erie, Ont. L2A 5X3

Chapter One

Bam!

The storage room door slammed shut, drowning Deputy U.S. Marshal Beauregard—Beau—Logue in inky blackness.

"Ms. Sherwood?" he called out, adrenaline pumping and body on full alert as a pathetically weak overhead bulb blinked on. "You all right?"

Nothing.

Not giving a damn what happened to the wine-glasses he'd been hauling for the petite, nearly eight months pregnant, proverbial Georgia peach, Beau dumped them clinking to his feet, then scrambled for the exit.

"Ms. Sherwood, talk to me!" Hand on the door-knob, shoulder bearing down on the door, Beau shoved with all his might, but it didn't budge. Someone had to have deliberately blocked it. "Ms. Sherwood? Gracie?"

Still nothing.

Not even a frick-frackin' mouse squeak.

And wouldn't you know it, he'd left his handheld radio in the restaurant's main dining room. Hadn't even felt the need for his headset, seeing how the operation thus far had been smooth.

Now what?

Had Chef Gracie's escapee ex-husband gotten to her? A couple of his hired guns? Was she sick? Passed out? She'd seemed fine just a second ago, but he knew from bitter experience pregnant women had issues.

Beau again rammed the door with his shoulder, but all he got for his efforts was crazy, red-hot pain.

"Okay, think, man. Think." Hands braced on his hips, he'd kept his head for all of two seconds when he tried punching the door. The only thing that netted was hurt knuckles, so he switched to Plan B—which pretty much consisted of a helluva lot of hollering.

"Yo, Mason! Mulgrave! Wolcheck! Anyone out there?"

No response. He moved on to Plan C.

The building was in the heart of Fort McKenzie's historic Gas Light District, meaning the restaurant occupied three older structures that used to be row houses in the trendy mountain town just an hour's commute to Portland, Oregon. The result was a hodgepodge of too narrow rooms and passages that'd no doubt barely passed city inspections.

All closed up like the place was, the air on this un-characteristically hot mid-August Tuesday morning was sticky. Smelled like the moldy sneakers he used for mowing his fixer-upper house's lawn.

Eyeing a putty knife on a shelf lined with grimy tools, he used it to wedge up and under the door's hinge pins. The top one popped right off. The second was rusty, but with teeth gritted, he worked that one free, as well. Beau managed to keep the heavy door steady long enough to lift it out of his way and lean it against the nearest shelves.

From his shoulder holster, he pulled his gun, readying it for whatever awaited behind the newly liberated door that, sure enough, someone had pad-locked a steel bar in front of.

He ducked under it.

In the now dark hall, he wasn't sure what to ex-pect—sure as hell not a convenient bread crumb trail—but what he got was exactly squat. He made a quick sweep of the area but found not so much as a long, blond hair for a clue.

For all practical purposes, Gracie Sherwood had vanished.

Not only did that tick Beau off because he took his job of protecting witnesses very seriously, but also he'd taken an instant liking to Ms. Sherwood. She was sweet, brave, defenseless. Reminded him of his good friend and fellow marshal Chance Mul-grave's wife who'd had it rough when her first husband had been killed right about the time she'd discovered she was pregnant.

With slumped shoulders, Beau made the long walk out to join the rest of his crew, radioing for the two guys patrolling the building's side and rear to come up front.

"Don't suppose any of you have seen Ms. Sherwood?" he asked once all were assembled.

Villetti chuckled. "You're kidding, right?"

Jaw clenched, Beau sighed. "It look like I'm kidding? Mason, Wolcheck, do me a favor and check the garage down the street for her car."

Five minutes later, the two guys were back.

Gracie Sherwood's car wasn't there.

What did it mean? Someone took her in her own vehicle?

Beau's stomach clenched.

Sure, it was possible, but more likely, for whatever oddball reason, he'd been duped. She'd used her Southern charm and curls to lure him into the storage closet. She'd locked him in, then taken off. But why? What did she know that he didn't that had her running? Was she joining her husband? Or running scared from him and thinking she'd be safer on her own?

"So what happened?" his younger brother Adam asked. "Hear signs of a struggle?"

"Not a peep."

"What're you gonna do?" Bug, Adam's best bud and the only woman on the team, asked. "This was a mighty high profile case for the boss. He finds out you're the one who *misplaced* her, well—" She finished her sentence with a low whistle that pretty much said it all.

No matter the cost, no matter where the hunt took him, Beau had to get Gracie Sherwood back—*now*. Not just for her, but himself. He'd already lost one pregnant woman. No way would he lose another.

FIFTEEN MINUTES after making her big escape, Gracie Sherwood—she'd long ago ditched her married name of Delgado in favor of her maiden surname— pulled her whale of a vintage pink Caddie convertible up to a convenience store gas pump. While her car guzzled gas, she counted money—or rather, her lack thereof: $184.32.

Not good, especially considering the cost of this one fill-up. Still, the $150 in the restaurant safe had been all she could get her hands on. The $34.32 all that was left of Vicente's now frozen assets. Not that she'd even want to spend a dime more of his money, but in this case, it would've at least been nice to have the option.

Inside, she made a quick trek to the ladies' room, paid for the fuel, a pack of mini powdered-sugar doughnuts, a banana and jug of OJ, then climbed back behind the wheel.

She tried finding a decent radio station, but this far out of Portland, got nothing but static. A week earlier, some punk had broken her car's antennae. The final nail in the coffin of a particularly rotten year.

Finding out the sophisticated, articulate, Harvard-educated Bolivian she'd fallen wildly in love with had in fact been up to his neck in the kinds of dirty dealing she couldn't even begin to comprehend had been hard to take. What'd happened after that nearly destroyed her.

Muggy, hot summer wind in her hair, she focused on the winding mountain road. Gracie ignored the latest lump in her throat and tightened her grip on the wheel.

With Vicente behind bars, she'd thought she'd been safe—at least until a month from now when her testimony would've forced her to face him at the trial. Lucky for her, she'd been the one to find his business log, onto the pages of which he'd meticulously recorded each illegitimate business dealing he'd been involved in. Everything from drug dealing to illegal importing to murder. All carefully documented in the event he'd ever needed to blackmail one of his associates. His ego was the size of Vermont, so knowing Vicente, he'd never even imagined it being found—let alone, used against him.

Although she was a week shy of eight months pregnant, she was now on her way to the Culinary Arts Invitational, held in just under two weeks in San Francisco. After she won the competition, Gracie planned on heading to her parents' home in Deerwood, Georgia.

As a master chef, she'd worked her whole life for this. Before finding out about Vicente, the hundred grand in prize money would've merely been icing on the cake of what she'd mistakenly believed had been her already fantastic life. Now that the restaurant she'd nurtured into a lucrative business had been closed due to nonexistent profits, since news about Vicente's dirty dealings had become public, the prize represented a second chance for her and her baby.

When she'd gotten the news Vicente had escaped, and that word on the street—according to Portland police—was that he was coming for her, at first she hadn't believed it.

But then, why not? she thought with a bitter laugh. The man had already committed an unspeakable crime against her. Why not finish her off?

After narrowly avoiding being abducted at gunpoint one afternoon while walking her neighborhood park, Gracie had gone back to the police, who'd turned her over to the U.S. Marshals' Witness Security Program.

She'd tried explaining to police about the competition soon to be held in San Francisco, how she had to be there, that it was the only way she'd ever get enough cash to start a new restaurant and life. But they'd said simply, no. She was too valuable a witness to let go.

A witness.

That's all she was to these guys.

They didn't see the pain she'd been through. The pain she was still working through. They didn't see the innocent baby girl she'd have to diaper with newspapers if she didn't win the top CAI prize. Yes, her parents would help best they could, but seeing how they were retired, it wasn't like they had a money tree shading their backyard.

Lucky for Gracie, the marshals who'd been sent to protect her had been even more chauvinistic, and thus easier to escape, than her husband's thugs.

She was sorry for having locked the nice one in the storage closet, but really, what else could she have done? From here on out, the nice marshal—along with the rest of his crew—were the enemy in the most important battle she'd ever fight.

The battle to regain her life. Her normalcy.

For many women, she supposed discovering their husband was a murdering psycho would probably ruin them. What happened after that…

No. It was in the past. Never to be spoken or thought of again. What was done was done, and she wasn't willing to become a slave to one horrific night.

Gracie had wanted to be a mother since she was three years old, playing with her Burp and Boo Betty doll. She'd dreamed of winning CAI's competition ever since her graduation from the prestigious Western Culinary Institute. With two such cherished goals on the line, no one—especially not some clueless marshal—was going to bring her down.

From here on out, she would take nice, deep breaths. Dream of holding her baby girl in her arms in the kitchen of the new restaurant the prize money would help start. In short, life would finally get back to normal.

Normal. The word had such a melodic sound. In a life led in *Normalville,* husbands didn't do what hers had. They didn't go to prison and then escape. They didn't want to kill pregnant wives.

Mmm…Gracie liked *Normalville.* Much preferred to her past locale of *Chaosville.* So she raised her face to the sun, pasted on a bright smile and reveled in the first unhurried, carefree moments of her and her baby's new lives.

"YOU SEEN HER?" Beau asked the clerk at the third convenience store he'd stopped at along Highway 26, the only route leading east or west out of Fort McKenzie. Other deputy marshals covered less traveled roads. He'd chosen this one for himself because if by chance Ms. Sherwood had gotten it in that pretty head of hers that she'd wanted to go for a nice drive home to Georgia—without her security detail—then by God, he'd be the one to give her a good talking to. The woman wasn't only putting her life at risk, but her baby's.

People who crossed Vicente Delgado died.

It was that simple.

His gut told him Gracie was too smart to have

gone back to hubby, which, after a quick look at her file, only left a couple other options. There was some cooking thing she'd told Portland PD she wanted to compete in, but after having been shot at, surely even she'd seen how attending such a well-publicized event was a bad idea. She had family in Georgia. But why would she want to drive all that way? No doubt it had something to do with her pregnancy. Best he could remember, women about to pop weren't supposed to fly, right?

The paunchy, graying Caucasian male manning the convenience store counter took the photo, eyed it a good fifteen seconds, then tapped it. "You know, I think I have seen her. Maybe an hour ago she got gas, then bought OJ and those little powdered sugar doughnuts. I remember 'cause the combination would've sent me to the ER with heartburn."

"Excellent," Beau said, snatching back the picture. "You see which way she went?"

"She definitely turned that pink tank of hers west."

West? Beau rubbed his throbbing forehead. Sighed.

Had she decided to go to that cooking thing after all? And if so, why? What didn't the woman get about psycho exes and crowds being a bad combination?

Well, soon as he caught up with her, he'd give her an education in both. Lucky for her, bad news exes were his specialty.

Climbing back in his SUV, grabbing Ray-Ban

Aviators from the dash and slipping them on, he couldn't help but wonder what was it with him and women?

When it came to judging guys, he could sniff a whack job from eighty miles back. Throw in a hot female, and his radar went haywire. Not that preggers Gracie Sherwood was either a whack job or hot—at least not in the conventional sense. But she was cute. And Lord knew, as in the case of his cheating ex-wife, cute had its own set of pitfalls.

Initially, when Gracie had first split, he'd been a little out of his mind. There. He'd admitted it. But he was stronger now. Her taking off wasn't anything like what had happened with Ingrid. Not even remotely. It was job stress making him crazy, linking everything into one big jumbo mess in his head. Time was all he needed to work through it. Everyone he knew agreed.

Now, all he had to do was convince himself.

"MA'AM?" Beau said to the waitress who'd just set a juicy double cheeseburger and fries on Gracie's table. Gracie was in the rest room. It was lunchtime at I-5, exit 282—about thirty minutes south of sweltering, traffic-clogged Portland. And while Beau was thrilled about having spotted Gracie's pink whale in the truck stop lot, then blocking her car in with his SUV, he was more thrilled about landing a burger. "Mind bringing me the same?"

"Sure," she said, giving him a funny look while he slid into the turquoise vinyl booth.

"Extra mayo and grilled onions, please."

"You got it."

In the meantime, Beau helped himself to Gracie's fries. Lucky for him, she'd chosen a lonely corner, away from the obnoxious pop blaring on the jukebox, out of the line of sight of anyone walking through the front door or on their way back from the john. Expecting Gracie to pounce the second she caught sight of him, Beau continued downing her fries, but remained on alert.

A few minutes later, she rounded the corner and gasped. "What're you—"

By the time Gracie had even realized what'd happened, a marshal—that nice one—stood, nudged her into the booth, then sat beside her, pinning her in. "Howdy," he said in his best Southern twang. "How *y'all* doin'?"

"Let me go," she snarled from between clenched teeth. "Or so help me, I'll scream so loud every redneck in this joint'll tear you to pieces."

"Good," Beau said, helping himself to another fry. "Then after that, they'll no doubt be happy to tackle the other guys after you."

"What *other* guys?"

"Four goons your hubby hired. Yesterday afternoon, a friend of mine from Portland PD gave me a tip. We found out that with the bulk of his pals still behind bars, your ex assembled a new crew to take you out. Which is why my boss feels a sense of urgency about getting you back under our protection."

"Right," Gracie said, snatching her plate from him, then wolfing down a fry. Oh, personal experience taught her Vicente was a man to be feared, but he wasn't superhuman. She wasn't using a credit card or cell phone, so as far as she knew, she couldn't be traced. As for how this marshal ended up finding her, she'd chalk that up to pure, dumb luck. She'd told police her plans to compete in San Francisco, and he no doubt assumed she'd be on I-5—the most direct route.

Mistake Number One.

From here on out, she'd stick solely to back roads.

After all, this close to obtaining her most cherished dreams of becoming a mother and winning the world renowned CAI competition, she wasn't about to do something stupid like put her life at risk.

Yes, Vicente no doubt knew that she would attend the Culinary Olympics, but come on, the man was a prison escapee. He was also brilliant. Meaning, he wouldn't risk freedom by showing up at one of the most publicized events in the culinary world.

Wishing for her own wafer-thin, home cooked potato chips accompanied by a nice, mellow dill dip, a turkey burger and side of pasta salad, Gracie instead made lemonade from the lemons of her life by grabbing for the ketchup bottle. But it was new, and the lid wouldn't budge.

The marshal calmly took the bottle from her, easily twisting off the top. It made a cheerful little pop.

Glaring at him, choosing to ignore the super-charged hum that'd passed between them when their hands brushed, Gracie took the bottle back, giving it a good, hard shake. She was just about to reach for her knife to stick it inside, when he took the bottle again, thumping the side and bottom with the heel of his hand.

Once a thick, red river of ketchup pooled on her plate, he calmly put the lid on the bottle, then reached past her to set it alongside a squeeze mustard bottle, sugar and napkins.

"I could've done that," she said, blocking his all-male scent of leather and cars and some other intriguing something she couldn't begin to identify, but had the craziest urge to explore. "I'm a chef. I have my own ketchup trick."

"Did I say you *couldn't* have done it?"

"No, but your tone implied it."

"What tone?"

"That one," she said, plucking pickles from her burger. "You used it just now. It plainly said you think I'm incompetent, and that I need a big, strong man to look after me and make my ketchup come out. But you know what? I made it this far on my own, and—" Startled, she jumped.

"Here you go," the waitress said, having caught Gracie off guard when she'd abruptly rounded the corner. She set a plate loaded with another burger and fries on the table. "Need anything else?"

"No, thank you," Gracie said. Why, oh why, when she'd flinched, hadn't she headed for the wall instead of her assigned marshal? Who actually, now that she'd gotten a better look at him, was disturbingly hot. The whole right side of her body still tingled.

But there were no tingles in *Normalville!* Especially when she had no want nor need for *any* men in her life—let alone hot ones!

"Actually," the marshal said to the waitress, "I wouldn't mind a Coke when you get a second."

"Be right back." On her return trip to the kitchen, the rail-thin redhead sang along with the jukebox.

"Mind passing the ketchup?" the marshal asked.

"I know what you're thinking," Gracie said, careful to set the stupid bottle in front of him, rather than risk another touching encounter by passing it directly into his waiting hand. "How if I'm skitterish enough to jump when a waitress comes around, that I must be a real head case. But I'll have you know I didn't flinch just a second ago because I was scared or nervous or anything. Flinching is a natural reaction often encountered during the latter stages of a woman's third trimester."

"Uh-huh," he said before taking a bite of his burger.

"You don't believe me?"

He just sat there chewing.

She cut her burger in half, then took a bite, only to wince before swallowing. "I can't eat this," she said.

"Why?"

"It's cold. I don't usually eat foods like…" Making a face, she waved at the offensive burger. "Plus, I have a texture issue about cold grease. Feels funny on my tongue."

"Take mine," he said, switching plates. "It's still good and hot."

"I couldn't," she said.

"Afraid I've got cooties? Want me to cut off the part where I bit?"

"Of course not," she said. And to prove it, she took a bite right beside his, only to then wish she'd have just stuck with her own cold burger.

The slow grin he cast her way made a mess of her earlier assumption that the man was her enemy. How long had it been since someone was truly nice to her? Sacrifice-his-own-hot-burger nice? A while. But that didn't mean now she should suddenly go soft.

If she let this marshal take her back to Portland, she'd be stuck in some so-called safe house for who knew how long before Vicente's case went to trial. Seeing how now that he'd vanished, he couldn't exactly be put on the stand. Her chance for winning the CAI's prize would be gone, along with her and her baby girl's future.

Keeping this in mind, she concentrated on finishing her marshal's burger and planning a new escape.

She'd tried living in *Chaosville* and found it not to her liking.

"Hate to interrupt you," she said while he downed the last of her burger. "But I've got to go to the bathroom."

"Again?" He sighed.

"Sorry." She flashed him her brightest smile. "Another pregnancy thing."

"It's okay," he said, sliding out of the booth. "But just in case you're thinking of trying anything, I'm going with you. Not only are you a key witness, but whether you want to acknowledge it or not, you're in danger."

"That's just plain silly," she said, thickening her accent. "Vicente would *nevuh* really hurt me. And now that you've found me, where could I possibly go? Now, be a good boy and please hand me my purse."

He cautiously did as she'd asked.

"Thank you. I won't be but a second."

"That's mighty considerate of you, *darlin'*, but just in case you get a hankering to take another drive, how about leaving me your keys?"

"Y-you can't be serious," she said. "After hearing about those other men trailing me, you honestly think I'd willingly leave your side?"

"Keys." He held out his hand, wagged his fingers.

With a huffy sigh, she dug through her purse, handing them to him.

"Thanks."

"You're not welcome."

While Gracie headed for the ladies' room, Beau sat on the opposite side of the booth so he could have a better view. He chuckled to recall the expression on her face when he'd asked for her keys. Boy, he'd really caught her off guard with that one. Of course she'd been planning another escape. Running straight for that cooking thing.

Seeing her, being near her, brought to mind memories of how things had been with Ingrid. The luminescence of pending motherhood. The luster of her hair. The rattler-type snap when coming between her and her food. How long had it been since he'd recalled happy memories about that time?

Still grinning, Beau shook his head.

The waitress approached. "Need any pie?"

"You know," Beau said, "that'd really hit the spot. Got anything chocolate?"

"Chocolate cream guaranteed to curl your toes."

"In that case," he said with a wink. "Better get two. My friend doesn't like to share."

She laughed. "When it comes to pie, I don't blame her."

The pie came, and in Beau's case, went. The waitress had been right—it was damned good.

He eyed the bathroom. Gracie had been in there awhile. Should he call the waitress back over and ask her to check on his Southern belle?

He did just that.

And when the redhead returned with a funny look, telling him the ladies' room was empty, if Beau had had three legs he would've kicked himself all the way back to Portland. How could he be so gullible?

How could Ms. Sherwood be so dumb?

He had her keys, so that left her sneaking away sometime during the thirty seconds in which he'd wolfed down his pie, then hitching a ride with a stranger. Surely he came across as more trustworthy than some of the scary-looking characters around here?

Leaving a twenty and ten on the table, Beau headed outside, shading his eyes against blinding sun.

Heat hovered in undulating waves above the blacktop. Not the best weather for a pregnant lady to be out hitching a ride.

The lot looked quiet. Three semis. Two off, one with the engine idling, stinking up the place with diesel exhaust. An assortment of eleven passenger cars lined the restaurant's front. Two more passenger cars were filling up at covered gas tanks. On the access road running alongside I-5, a silver minivan whizzed by.

Beau looked to his own vehicle, to the big, pink Caddie, he'd blocked—

What the?

Gracie's car was gone. The bushes in front of it flattened. His SUV's grill all busted to hell. She'd even stabbed his driver's side front tire. He knew it had been her because of the pink-handled metal nail file still stuck in the rubber.

When had she given him the slip? While he'd ordered pie? Common sense told him the bathroom's location meant it was an interior room with only one exit. How was it a chirpy blonde who had tongue issues with cold grease had so effortlessly gotten away from him not once, but twice?

And how long was it going to take for him to get his tire patched so he could once and for all teach Gracie Sherwood who was boss?

More importantly, how long until he finally got it through his head that just because Gracie was pregnant, that didn't mean he owed her special favors. He'd bent over backward trying to be kind to his wife, and look where that'd left him. He still hadn't been able to right the wrong between them. The even sadder truth was that even if he'd wanted to, there was nothing he could've done.

Chapter Two

"Listen up," Beau said to Gracie through a still chain-locked door, six frick-frackin' hours later, standing on the covered porch of a kitschy, roadside motel just south of Oregon's Bandon State Park. Surrounded by a brooding fir forest, the brown and gray strip motel with plywood castle towers on either end and a moat-shaped pool with more moss than water looked like some Brothers Grimm fairy tale gone wrong.

It was only seven at night, yet in the shadows, felt more like midnight.

Gracie had parked her pink Caddie in front of her room.

Odds were, Beau never would've found her without a tip from a local cop who'd spotted her car. The man had offered his assistance in bringing Gracie in, but after her latest slip, for Beau anyway, this case had gotten personal. Or maybe it had always been personal, he thought, swiping his fingers through his hair.

Seeing how the rest of the crew was scattered at least a hundred miles in all different directions, looked like he had the good fortune to be bringing Ms. Sherwood in all by himself. "It's time you learned who's leading this mission. There are a lot of things I'll put up with, but this hide-and-seek game's getting old, and—" What was that funny noise?

Was she crying?

Oh, man, if his momma had still been alive to see this, she'd thump him upside his head. His dad still could, for making this little bitty pregnant thing sob.

Ingrid never once cried. Not during the entirety of her cruelly sterile speech.

"T-that's so—wait," Gracie said, noisily unhooking the chain. "I can't even speak." Whatever kind of girly cry she had going, it grew steadily worse until Beau felt two inches tall. On his list of things he didn't do, making women cry was at the top. "Oh my gosh, you're funny. Thanks. I haven't had a belly laugh like that in—well, since never. At least not in the recent past."

Funny? She called that donkey braying laughter? At his expense?

Door open, he brushed past her and stormed into the room, wanting for some unfathomable reason to be put off by peeling, smoke-stained wallpaper and the busted-tile bathroom usually indicative of this sort of hole-in-the-wall establishment. What he got was a scene from *Southern Living*—MTV style.

She'd draped silky-looking scarves over lamps, lending the place an exotic glow. The germy motel bedspread had been replaced with faux fur. Mink? On top of that were a half-dozen pillows, all embroidered with quirky sayings like, *Woman cannot live on chocolate alone...She needs shopping, too!*

As if all of that wasn't enough, the smell was... fantastic? Some heavenly concoction simmering on a two-burner kitchenette stove sent his ravenous stomach into a growling fit. Too bad he was here to drag her back to Portland and not to eat!

"You haul all of this stuff around with you?" he asked.

Stepping inside, Gracie shut the door. His one question turned her smile upside down. "This *stuff*, my cooking gear and a few clothes were all I brought into my marriage, so that's all I took when it was over."

"Sure," he said with a nod.

"Sure?" She shook her head. "I tell you my life is over, and that's all you have to say?"

She'd paraded spicy-smelling candles across the top of the TV, and he sliced his finger through the flames. "Sorry. But that doesn't change the fact that you're returning to Portland with me. *Now.*"

"No."

"Excuse me?"

"I'm exhausted. I've been driving all day. I still have a couple more sauce variations to try tonight. If

you insist on dragging me back, I'll go peaceably—
but in the morning."

"Fair enough," he said, but was he a fool for taking
her at her word?

Suddenly, standing there, looking at her, there
wasn't enough air in the room. Her candles and the
rich sauce were eating it all.

The size of her stomach and glow of her skin were
similar to Ingrid's, but that's where the resemblance
ended. Ingrid had been out for Ingrid. Period. But
Gracie, this drive of hers to win a contest was all for
the sake of her baby—so that he or she could live a
better life. A safer life. Beau admired the hell out of
her. And wanted to know more about her than the
bland fare found in her file.

"If you have to stay," she said, "you might as well
make yourself at home." She was back in the tiny yet
workable kitchen, dumping pasta she'd had bubbling
on the back burner into a colander she'd already set
in the sink. "The TV only gets five channels, but I
guess that's better than nothing."

He shrugged.

Had she always been so pretty? Had so many
curls? She'd cupped her hands to her big belly, cast
him a half grin that lit her whole face. He wanted to
stay mad at her, but she was like a too cute kitten—
only she wasn't a cat, but a woman. Had she been a
cat, he would've just played with her. Stroked her fur
and scratched behind her ears. Just thinking about

what Gracie would do to him if he tried either of those activities made him smile.

His ex had been hard as nails. No petting allowed.

"Mind letting me in on the joke?" she asked, glancing over her shoulder while giving her brew a stir.

"Nah. But thanks for asking." He winked.

She frowned. "Fine. Don't tell me." Back to stirring, she hummed a soft, nonsensical tune.

"I won't."

"Why do you have to be so obstinate?" she asked, wiping her hands on an industrial-type white apron, then crossing the room to switch on the TV with a remote.

"Wasn't aware I was being anything."

"You're obviously uptight," she said, switching past news, *Wheel of Fortune* and an infomercial, finally landing on a black and white movie. "What you need is a good meal. A nice bottle of wine. You're all cranked up inside."

"Cranked up?"

"Yeah, you know, stressed out. Uptight. At the very least, have a seat, or else it's going to be a very long night."

"Already has been," he said, turning his back on her to peer behind curtains. All quiet save for his erratic pulse. If they were staying the night, he'd feel better if the cars were parked in back, out of casual sight. Odds were Vicente's goons were miles from here, but better safe than sorry.

"Anything exciting going on?" she asked from her perch on the foot of the bed. "Parades? A tailgate party?"

"Give me your keys," he said. "This time, your *car* keys."

"Oops," she said with a big, cheesy grin. "I'm bad."

"Yes, you are," he said. "So give me both sets."

"I'd be happy to if you'd be so kind as to hand me my purse."

He did, and she took her time fishing through the jangling contents, eventually catching two sets of keys, just as he'd requested.

"Here you go." She dangled them.

Finally some cooperation out of the woman.

"Just one more thing," he said. "Hate doing this, but in your case, it has to be."

From his jeans' back pocket, he withdrew cuffs.

"Oh, no," she said, scrambling back into the pillow pile. "No way you're cuffing me. I have to keep stirring my sauce. And anyway, I haven't done anything wrong."

"Are you kidding me? You've done *everything* wrong." Before she escaped again, he cuffed her left wrist, then secured the free cuff to the wall-mounted lamp. He hated doing this, hated using such a flimsy hold. Had she been a man—hell, if she hadn't been so pregnant and vulnerable looking—he wouldn't have thought twice about forcing her under the open kitchen sink counter to secure her to the pipes.

"I have every intention of testifying at my ex-husband's trial," she said. "But until then, I've got things to do. All I did in running from you was fight for my right to live life on my own terms. Is that so bad?"

"It is when you're putting that life at risk. Now, sit tight for about three minutes, then I'll free you. Look," he said, turning for the stove. "To prove I'm a nice guy, I'll even turn off the burner so whatever you're cooking doesn't burn."

"Lucky me," she said with a wag of her cuffed wrist. "Here I don't even know your name and you're already handy in the kitchen and getting kinky in bed."

"For the record," he said at the door, "I can get a lot kinkier than this. And the name is Beauregard Logue. Friends call me Beau."

"That mean we're friends?" she asked with a hopeful smile.

"You can call me, *Mister* Logue."

"No," Gracie said under her breath not five seconds after the beast strolled out the door. "I'll call you out of my life."

Easing upright, she used her free hand to turn off the lamp, unscrew the finial and remove the shade.

Ouch! The bulb was hot—took forever to get out seeing how she had to keep stopping for wince breaks. After yanking out the harp, freeing herself was a simple matter of lifting her arm eight inches.

Peering through the door's peephole, she watched Marshal Beau drive around back.

Once he was out of sight, she flew into action. Running out the front door to her car, then grabbing the spare key from the magnetic box she kept under the driver's side wheel well—she was awful about locking her keys in the car.

Now came the tricky part. Sure, she could head right back out on the road, but she'd be caught faster than she got gas after eating broccoli.

No, this time, she'd have to be more creative. And so instead of turning south on the highway, she turned north, pulling her car into an abandoned junkyard, camouflaging the pink in a sea of rust and primer gray. Thick, conifer-scented woods circled the cars, and in midday, she was sure the place had a quaint feel, but at the moment, she had a major case of the creeps.

She waited an hour in muggy dusk, the whole time swatting at whiny bugs until her entire body felt coated with grit and mosquito bites. Until dust and dirt ground between her teeth and she tasted it on her tongue. Only then, in rapidly fading daylight, did she figure it was safe to return to the motel for her stuff. Certainly Marshal Beau was long gone.

Everything that meant anything to her was in that room. Photos and diaries and recipes. Pricey pans and accoutrements. A few pieces of jewelry she hoped to pawn for the cash she'd need to get her the rest of the way to San Francisco. From there, her hotel room was prepaid, and with luck, she'd have the prize money to get her home.

She parked around back, trudged up to the front desk for another key, explaining to the clerk that she'd locked the first one in the room.

By the time she slipped the key into the lock, Gracie was beyond tired. Her feet were swollen, her lower back aching, and she could really have gone for a Caesar chicken salad and French onion soup. As for her cream sauce experiments, all she could do at this point was toss it all and start fresh wherever she stopped tomorrow.

In the room, she headed straight for the bathroom sink. It would take ten days to scrub all the junkyard grime from her face. She brushed her teeth, too. She needed a shower, but the mere thought seemed too energetic.

After securing her long mess of naturally curly hair in a scrunchie, she slipped off her shoes and headed for bed. Surely she'd feel better after a nice, long snooze?

Only after turning around and getting her first good look at the bed, she found that not only was her fuzzy faux-mink spread missing, but also the scarves she'd put over the lamps and her pillows and—she stormed to the bathroom. He'd even taken her ultra-fluffy pink towels and no, even he wouldn't have sunk that low…

Running for the suitcase she'd stashed in a small closet, she yanked open the door and couldn't have felt lower if the man had socked her in the stomach.

Shoulders sagging, the tears she'd been too stubborn to shed since the start of this whole ordeal finally spilled.

Her recipes.

The creep had taken her recipes—not only that, but also all of her cooking gear.

The CAI contest was unique in that you couldn't fully prepare before arrival. There were one hundred and ninety-three chefs, each representing the globe's countries—unlike the U.S., the CAI recognized Taiwan. In each of five rounds, the ethnic theme of her meals was determined by luck of the draw. She could draw Ethiopia. India. Greenland. In her recipe journal was years of research. Without it, she might as well not even go to San Francisco. What was the point when she didn't have a prayer of winning?

Jeez, her back hurt. And now, her head and heart.

Why had Marshal Beau done this?

How could he be so cruel?

She sat hard on the foot of the bed, cradling her forehead in her hands.

Who was she trying to kid? Vicente's capture had been big news. His spectacular prison break even bigger. As his ex-wife, the woman carrying his baby, Gracie had been in the news right along with him. For all she knew, the world-renowned Culinary Arts Institute might have rescinded her invitation without even letting her know. Hers was a type of publicity they didn't want.

On the flip side, she owed it to this tiny life growing inside to at least try.

Freeing her hands to rub her bulging tummy, she looked up toward the dresser and TV. Sitting beneath her favorite bottle of perfume—the only non-essential item left in the room—was a note written on a yellow legal pad.

> Want your stuff? Let's make a deal.
> Meet me at the Fish Tale Motel
> in Orick, California. Noon tomorrow.
> —Your Fave Marshal.

Instead of the customary signature at the bottom of his note, he'd drawn a smiling stick guy bearing a star-shaped badge on his chest. Of all the nerve…

He'd stolen everything she owned and thought she'd be happy about it? Oh—she'd meet him all right, but if he thought for one second she'd peaceably return to Portland with him, he had about as much brain power as his stupid, smiling stick man!

"'BOUT TIME *y'all* got here," Marshal Beau said with a slow grin and that infuriating imitation of her accent. Granted, she'd poured it on thick the morning she'd locked him in that storage closet, but it hadn't been *that* thick.

"Where's my property?" she asked from behind the wheel, shading her eyes against blinding noon sun. Their appointed meeting spot was an even more tired establishment than the last one she'd stayed at.

The Fish Tale Motel was on the outskirts of the bustling tourist town of Ulmstead—located in the heart of redwood country. The towering redwood setting was spectacular, sweet-scented and warm; it was almost enough to make the giant log cabin, with its tattered green roof, charming. An abandoned mini-waterslide had been filled with pungent yellow marigolds.

"Get out," Marshal Beau said, "then I'll show you."

"If it's all the same to you, I'd just as soon you put it in my trunk."

"And then you drive off into the sunset?"

She laughed. "It's high noon. There's a ways to go before nightfall."

"You know what I mean." He braced his hands on the side of her door. Strong hands, with long elegant fingers. His muscular forearms were tan, a few light hairs mixed among the dark, glinting in the sun.

Yes, she thought, licking her lips. A few seconds earlier she'd known exactly what he'd meant, but somewhere between his biceps and broad shoulders, she'd totally lost track of her thoughts.

"Get out," he said. *"Please."*

She sighed. "You, *please*, cut me some slack. I feel eighteen months pregnant, according to you, my husband's trying to kill me and I haven't had a decent meal in two days."

"Wait just a sec," Beau said, jogging the fifteen feet to his black SUV.

He soon headed back her way bearing a large grocery sack. "This is for you," he said, "but only if you'll at least get out long enough to talk to me."

"I'm not stupid," she said, thumping her forehead against the steering wheel. "I get out, you'll slap cuffs on me. That'll be it. My whole life instantly ruined."

"Look—" he knelt, resting his forearms on her door "—I'll level with you. You're not going to like it, but for your own good, it has to be said."

"What?" She made the mistake of raising her head to meet his eyes. They were amazing eyes. Deep walnut with flecks of mossy-green. Above all, they were kind, not the eyes of a man deadset on destroying her life.

"Gracie Sherwood, this isn't a game. Your ex-husband wants to kill you—and your baby."

"I have to get to that competition," she said, refusing to let his words sink in. "And anyway, how would Vicente or his supposed hired thugs ever even find me?"

"I did. You're a looker, driving a *look-at-me* car. Believe me, you're not too hard to find."

"Then why'd you have to steal my stuff to get me back?"

"I didn't," he said. "All I had to do was temporarily store your belongings in my car, then wait. I knew it was just a matter of time till you returned."

"So all night and day you've been right behind me?"

"Pretty much."

"Who else?"

He looked away.

"Tell me."

"So far, one suspicious guy in a forest-green Hummer."

"And?" she asked, looking toward the busy highway. "Where is he now?"

"He, ah, turned off around Fort Dick."

"Uh-huh. Which only proves my point that Vicente's no fool. He wants nothing more to do with me. What happened back in Portland was no doubt some last chance, desperation effort designed to scare me, which it did. I've left town—for all my ex knows, for good."

Marshal Beau sighed. "Ever heard that saying about the calm before the storm? Right now, you happen to be in the sun—and I'm not complaining, but your ex isn't known for being a warm, fuzzy kind of guy. If you come with me now, you'll have a team of folks to keep you safe. If not…" He shrugged.

She bravely raised her chin. "I guess, seeing how I'm safe for the moment, I'll pick, *not*."

Chuckling, he said, "Actually it's *not* up for negotiation. I was trying to be nice, but—"

Nice? Gracie didn't have time for nice, so she grabbed for the bag bearing what she prayed were doughnuts, then gunned her engine. She might not get much of a lead, and hot Marshal Beau might still have her stuff, but the way she saw it, desperate times called for desperate measures. She had to get to San Francisco. Winning that contest was her and her baby's only shot at a decent future.

BEAU PRESSED OFF his cell phone, sick after having to admit to the boss that he'd lost Gracie—again. Only this time, it really wasn't his fault, but that of fierce tourist traffic. He'd kept up with her no problem for thirty miles, then at Steed Point, he'd been cut off by a gang of parading preschoolers on tricycles celebrating Clean Air Day.

From there on, it was slow going. Checking every dirt crossroad for rising dust, signaling she might've gone off the main path. In every town he approached, he checked every gas station, restaurant and motel for her car—as did the other marshals assigned to the case.

It was ten that night when he got the call from Adam that they'd found her in an inland motel. "Want me to cuff her and bring her in?"

Resting his forehead on the steering wheel, Beau sighed.

At this point, he wasn't sure what to do.

God only knew why, but he had a soft spot for the woman. She'd proven herself to be a major pain in his derriere, but seeing how she was pregnant and all, he at least wanted her treated with kid gloves. She had a goal, which was way more than he could say for himself.

Sure, he had his career, but it wasn't enough. Not nearly enough. For as long as he could remember, he'd wanted a real family. Like the one he'd grown up in only better, because his future wife, the mother of his children, wasn't going to die like his own mom had.

In marrying Ingrid, he'd thought himself well on his way to making his every dream come true. Funny how that so-called dream had turned nightmare.

"Yeah," he said to his brother, "I guess if it comes down to it, go ahead and cuff Gracie, but be gentle. I don't want her or the baby getting hurt."

"Duh," Adam said. "When's the last time I banged up a—" His brother's sudden silence hit Beau hard. It was tough enough on Beau remembering what'd happened to the last woman Adam had been assigned. Beau couldn't imagine how his brother must feel. Yeah, he had woman problems, but at least Ingrid was still alive.

"What happened to Angela wasn't your fault," he told Adam for the hundredth time. "Could've happened to any one of us. Now, with Gracie, just use common sense. She's an itty-bitty thing. Crafty, but she doesn't bite."

"Bro," Adam said an hour later just as Beau approached the miniscule town of Boynton where

Gracie had finally been found. "You're not gonna believe this, but she got away again."

"How?" Beau asked.

"I was just about to slap cuffs on her, when she bit me!"

AT FOUR in the morning, while everyone else on the team had long since pulled over for naps, Beau was still out looking. For sure, Vicente's new crew wasn't sleeping. If they got to Gracie before him, well…

Beau refused to think about it.

It was four thirty-seven by the digital clock on his dash when he pulled into the rear of a relic of a motel with individual cabins for rooms. On the outskirts of the Mendocino National Forest, the place was surrounded by more of the dark, eerie, dense forest that was starting to be a major pain in his ass when he spotted Gracie's car behind the last unit.

He killed his lights and engine a few cabins back. Took his time getting out of his car, rolling his shoulders, trying to work out Gracie-induced kinks.

Every cabin save for one was dark, so he headed toward Cabin Eight with its bluish TV glow.

When she'd been little, and sick or upset from a bad day at school, his sister Gillian had liked to fall asleep in front of the living room TV.

Maybe Gracie was the same?

He peered through the inch or so between the curtain and wall. A lone man sat up in bed, sipping a Coors.

Great. Now what?

Beau yawned. Rubbed his eyes. Headed for the motel office.

Of course, at this time of the morning it was closed, but he wailed on the bell regardless.

"I'm comin', I'm comin'." A wisp of an elderly woman who didn't at all match her booming, gravelly voice flicked on lights in a shabby reception area. "You want me to open the door," she shouted through thin glass, "show me you got money for a room."

"How much?" Beau asked.

"Forty."

He flashed two twenties.

She unlocked the door.

"I'll need your license," she said from behind a counter she could barely see over.

"Here's the thing," he said, setting the cash on the counter. "My wife is already here, so I'll just need the number of her room."

The clerk raised her eyebrows.

"She forgot to charge her cell, otherwise, I'd just call."

Tapping a vintage black rotary-dial parked beside his left elbow, she said, "Here you go. Each cabin has its own line. Only one single gal girl staying with us tonight." She wrote a number on a pad that said Alpine Lodge across the top.

Beau flashed his star, then smiled. "You know, I

really hate waking her. How about you *please* tell me which cabin is hers."

"How do I know that badge is real? For all I know, you bought it off the Web. You could be some serial killer."

Beau sighed. "Never mind, ma'am. Thank you for your time."

He turned to leave.

"Take your money. I don't deal with any of you late-night sickos."

Tucking the money in his wallet, Beau headed back out into the night.

One by one, he knocked on cabin doors. "Housekeeping!"

"Get a life, bud!"

"Maintenance! I've gotta unplug your john!"

"Screw you!"

Five doors later, a cop pulled into the dirt lot, lights and siren blazing.

"Good girl," Beau said under his breath about the desk clerk he'd apparently correctly pegged as the type to call the law on him.

"Freeze!" the cop said, gun and flashlight aimed at Beau as he emerged from his car. "Okay, now slowly raise those hands."

Wincing from the blinding light, Beau did as he'd been told.

Glancing off to his left and right, out of the light's glare, he saw that just as he'd hoped, lamps flicked on and draperies parted in all but cabins Three and Fifteen. The former had been the one Gracie's tank was parked closest to, so Beau deduced Cabin Three was hers.

The cop asked, "Mind telling me what you're doing out this hour of the night, knocking on sleeping citizens' doors?"

Beau said, "I'm a deputy U.S. Marshal down from Portland."

"Right." Rolling his eyes, the cop said, "And I'm Santa. Let's see some ID."

Beau obliged, and five minutes later, after the officer made a few calls and found his story checked out, Beau was free to go.

"Ho, ho, ho," the now jovial cop said. "Sorry to rain on your parade."

"Not a problem," Beau said.

Once he was again alone, and all those lamps had gone out, Beau trudged to Cabin Three.

He gave Gracie the benefit of a courtesy knock, then worked magic on the lock with equipment he didn't officially have.

Inside, he quietly shut the door.

Gracie was sitting up in bed, hands curved around her bulging stomach, looking prettier, softer, more fragile than she ever had.

For an instant he looked away, hating to think himself the cause of her grim expression. If only she'd get it through that thick head of hers that he wasn't the problem, but the solution.

"I'm so tired of this," she said softly. And she did look tired. Even in the dim light leaking in from the Alpine Lodge's blue neon sign, he saw circles under her eyes. "Can't we just be friends?"

"I wasn't aware we weren't."

She sighed. "Come on, Beau. Enough games."

"We're now on a first-name basis?"

"You know what I mean."

"Yeah," he said, drawing the room's one chair up to the head of the bed. "I do."

"So then this is it? You agree to let me go on to San Francisco? Alone?"

He laughed.

"This isn't funny, damn you, it's my life."

"I'm not disputing that."

"Then why are you acting this way? Like my wanting to take my hard-earned spot in a prestigious competition is wrong? I mean think about it, this is the Olympics for cooks. People kill for chances like…" As her words trailed off, she tucked her lower lip into her mouth.

"Oh man," he said with a groan. "You're not going to cry, are you?"

"Maybe." She looked up, slaying him with her baby blues. Only in this light, he couldn't even really see them, just a shimmer. It was only in his mind those eyes could hurt him. And because he knew that, because he was savvy to her every trick, he pulled his cuffs from his back pocket and slapped one on her wrist.

This time, she laughed, only it wasn't at all funny sounding, but laced with raspy tears. "I was trying to be serious. You know, open up. But it's obvious you couldn't care less how I feel. All you care about is getting your man."

"Yeah, but you're a woman," he said. All woman. Which was why he had to stay strong.

"I'm not going to run again," she said.

"I know."

Her face brightened in a smile so hopeful, so lovely and pure that it clenched his gut with ridiculous desires. Silly stupid things like wanting to hold her and protect her and beat the crap out of anyone who dared ruin her pregnancy's peace. "Does that mean you finally trust me? That you agree I should do the competition?"

"No."

"Then what? It has to mean something that you finally believe I'm done running."

"Oh." He flashed her a slow grin. "It means something, all right." He slapped his free cuff on his own wrist. "Means you can run all you want, but wherever you go, this time, I'll be with you."

Chapter Three

Beau groaned.

Gracie was crying. Big 'ol messy Southern belle tears just a little too over the top to be convincing.

When she got to the point in her show where she gazed up at him, batting long, tear-fringed eyelashes glinting in the light spilling in from the parking lot, he yanked the hand cuffed to her to his free one, flooding the now-silent room with bawdy applause. "Woo-hoo!"

He threw in an ear-splitting whistle, too.

"You're a beast," she spat, trying to roll over, taking him along for the ride.

"Hey—my arm doesn't bend that way, thank you very much."

"And I wasn't crying for your entertainment pleasure, thank *you* very much!"

"Look, lady, how about we agree to disagree and call it a night?"

"I would, but I'm cold. I can't sleep without my faux mink throw."

"So you're wanting me to uncuff you long enough to go get it?"

"Yes, please."

He sighed. Ran his palm over the day and night's stubble on his jaw. "Tell you what, you want that ratty old thing that bad, I'll be happy to walk outside *with* you to get it from my trunk."

"But I'm tired and my ankles are swollen."

"Me, too—on both counts." He stood, yanked her arm sideways to allow himself the range of motion needed to jerk the spread off the extra bed, then the blanket. After lying down beside her, then covering them both, he growled, "Night."

"I'm supposed to just lay here flat like this? I don't have enough pillows, and when my head isn't high enough, I always wake with heartburn."

"Here," he said, yanking his own pillow out from under his head to awkwardly ram it under hers.

"Thank you."

"Yeah."

After a few moments' blessed silence, Beau was finally nodding off when she sighed.

Instantly, he was awake. "What?"

"I'll never be able to sleep like this. If only I could—"

"Roll over."

"What?"

"If I have to tell you again, I'll roll you myself."

She rolled, his arm flailed up at an awkward as

hell angle, and because above all he was a gentlemen, not about to have this very pregnant woman accuse him of not having gotten adequate rest on his watch, he somehow managed to fall asleep.

Staying asleep was a whole other matter.

"Quit," he mumbled when something kept rubbing his wrist.

"Huh?"

"Whatever you're doing, knock it off."

"I'm just laying here, trying to—"

"That! That little movement right there suspiciously close to Chinese water torture."

"That?" She giggled. "That's the baby, silly. She's a night owl. Watch…" She flicked on the wall-mounted lamp on her side of the bed, then rolled onto her back and flung off the blanket. "Just keep your eyes on my belly, and—there! Did you see that?"

"Damn, that was pretty cool. Will he do it again?"

"*She*. And probably. Just keep watching."

He or she did do it again—and again.

Watching that all-too-familiar show did something to Beau. As did seeing the wisp of a smile curving the corners of Gracie's lips. She was proud of this baby—and she had a right to be. As he'd thought many times with Ingrid, having something that big moving around in your gut didn't look all that comfortable.

"Does it hurt?" he asked with the next alienlike rise in her stomach.

"Not at all," she said. "More like tickles."

Well, that was good news.

"I hope this turns out right for you," he said.

"Me, too."

He made the mistake of meeting her big, blue stare, shimmering with unshed tears. A mysterious something in his own gut told him this time, her emotion was the real deal. And he hated that he was the one making her cry.

In the vast majority of his experiences with women, usually it turned out the other way around. Them making him cry. Not that he'd actually boo hooed—just that he'd felt miserable enough that if he'd been of the crying persuasion, the night Ingrid dumped him for that stodgy partner of hers would've been a legitimate tear-worthy occasion.

It turned out the child she'd carried for the past seven months, the child he'd been celebrating as his own for the past seven months, wasn't really his, but her partner's.

After that, how many times had he wished life's tables could be turned? That he could be the one causing angst in a relationship? But now, even though this could hardly be called a romantic circumstance, he didn't like the thought of Gracie for real crying one little bit.

A duo of tears slid down her left cheek. Purely on reflex, he brushed them away.

"You're not going to let me go, are you?"

Lips pressed tight, he shook his head.

"That sucks," she said. "But I guess you're just doing your job."

"Trying," he said. "But if it's any consolation, I'm not enjoying this any more than you." In fact, being forced up against her like this, her lush curves spread before him like a veritable smorgasbord of womanhood, his assignment was growing harder by the second—quite literally. As best he could, he shifted his fly, trying his damnedest to ignore the canyon of heat scorching his legs, chest and shoulder where their bodies touched.

"Good," she said, casting him a sarcastic smile much more indicative of the woman who'd locked him in a storage closet. Thank God. If she'd maintained her softer side, he'd have been in real trouble.

"Ready for some sleep?" she asked.

Yeah. Oh, hell yeah.

She turned off the light, pulled the blanket back up over her. He braced himself for her roll, and sure enough, there it was. With his arm back up at an awkward angle, his other elbow digging into his ribs, Beau closed his eyes and sighed, telling himself he'd slept in worse places at far worse angles.

Finally, finally, he'd drifted off to dreamland when—

"Marshal Beau?"

"Yes?"

The light switched on. "I *really* have to go to the bathroom."

"I'M NOT LEAVING MY CAR," Gracie said. Around ten the next morning the two of them stood in a chilly drizzle just outside her cabin.

She breathed deeply of fresh-washed, conifer-scented air, vowing today would be a great day. A normal day. Marshal Beau couldn't keep her cuffed forever. All she had to do was sit tight and plan another escape and she'd soon be back on her way.

Marshal Beau pulled the cabin's door shut. Gave her that look she was beginning to know and love. The one that said he was counting to ten in his head in a futile attempt to keep from strangling her. She knew the look because for the vast majority of the time they'd been together, she'd been doing the same with him.

"Ms. Sherwood, I've called a tow truck, and your car will be safely garaged back in Portland. Your belongings are in the back of my vehicle. I'm doing everything I can to be reasonable. Hell, I spent the whole night with my elbow up my ass trying to make you comfortable, but—"

"You don't have to be crude. I'm used to being around more refined men."

He snorted. "Oh, so let me see, all of the sudden, your convicted murderer, drug-dealing, scum of a husband is a great guy because he—"

Pa-ching!

"Shit!" he hollered, roughly grabbing her upper arm. "Get down."

"Why? What was that?"

"A bullet. Attached to a gun with a silencer. Come on." Crouching behind shrubs, he pushed her in front of him, then pulled a gun from a shoulder holster and started firing.

Pow! Pow! Pow!

"Oh my God, oh my God…" Gracie chanted the phrase over and over. "I didn't think any of this was real. That you were somehow just making it all up to get your way, but—"

"Please," he said, lacing the fingers of their cuffed hands, then giving her a squeeze. "Keep it together for me a little while longer."

"I can't, I can't, I—"

He kissed her. Hard. Fast. "You have to. Come on."

Pa-ching! Pa-ching!

"See that black SUV?" He pointed five cabins down.

"You kissed me," she said, fingertips to her lips.

He shook his head.

"Y-yes, yes, you did."

Pa-ching! Pa-ching! Pa-ching!

"For cryin' out loud, woman, it was just a kiss. It was the only way I could think to get your attention."

"You could've just slapped me," she hissed, still reeling from the shocking pleasure of him pressing his lips to hers.

"You'd have rather I—"

Pa-ching!

"W-what about the SUV?" she asked.

He fished for something from his front jeans

pocket, then pulled out a tiny key. "If I let you loose, promise to do the smart thing and run for that car?"

Pa-ching! Pa-ching!

She swallowed hard and nodded.

He unlocked the cuffs, and even though their hands were free, he squeezed her fingers again. "On three," he said.

She nodded.

"One…Two…Go!"

Gracie ran for all she was worth, her marshal close on her heels, firing back.

Pow! Pow! Pow!

Pa-ching! Pa-ching! Pa-ching! Pa-ching!

In the car, heart pounding, Gracie hunched down in her seat.

Seconds later, Beau hopped in beside her, slamming his door and starting the engine simultaneously.

"You okay?" he asked, revving the engine, throwing a rooster tail of gravel up behind them as he sped from the lot.

Afraid she couldn't speak past the wall of terrified tears blocking her throat, she nodded.

Pa-ching! Pa-ching!

"Beau! They're following! Hurry!"

"I'm doin' the best I can, darlin'. Put on your seat belt. I'd do it for you, but…"

Yeah, she could see he was kind of busy.

He careened onto a side street.

Seconds later, made a sharp right.

"Dammit," he mumbled. "They're still back there."

"At least they're not shooting."

Pa-ching!

"You were saying?"

"ON THE BRIGHT SIDE," Gracie said with a weak chuckle thirty minutes later, her breathing just now slow enough that she could speak without hyperventilating. "At least we lost my ex-husband's *associates*."

Stopped on the shoulder of a dirt road winding through forest so thick they might as well have been in a tunnel, her marshal thumped his forehead against the steering wheel. "Unfortunately with my cell not having a signal, we've also lost ourselves."

"Hey—you were the one driving. All I did was sit here screaming."

He'd had his eyes closed, but opened one long enough to glare at her. "Thanks."

Making the mistake of gazing out her window, Gracie found the woods looking tall, dark and spooky—like one of those Bigfoot documentaries on The Travel Channel. Primeval ferns lined the road, and the only sound aside from a faint whoosh high in the Douglas fir, western red hemlock and Sitka spruce was the occasional rapid-fire hammer of a woodpecker somewhere in the gloom.

Far off thunder rumbled.

Gracie shivered.

Goose bumps covered her forearms, which then made her have to pee. Bad.

Not a good thing considering there wasn't a rest area, gas station or McDonald's anywhere in sight.

"I really have to go to the bathroom," she said.

This time, Marshal Beau didn't even open one eye. He just sat there. Stone silent. Like the moss-covered boulders on the side of the road.

A sprinkle of fat raindrops hit the windshield, only worsening her need to pee.

"I'm not kidding," she said. "I've *reeaally* got to go. I'm sure this is too much information, but the baby's sitting on my bladder. I can only hold it for like twenty more seconds—tops."

Still nothing.

"Are you even listening to me?" She gave his shoulder a nudge. After which, he grunted before reaching for his side, revealing a dark, sticky substance all over the back of his navy marshal's jacket. It was on the seat, too. Smudging the black leather.

Hands to her mouth, she shook her head.

Had he been shot?

But when?

How could she not have noticed? He hadn't been bawling with pain or anything. He'd just driven her to safety, all the while he'd been sitting there bleeding to… No.

No bleeding to death in such an already creepy location. Especially when it was her fault he'd been shot. The whole time she'd been running from him, convinced he was only lying to get her back to Portland to testify, he'd been telling the truth—that she, and her baby—were in danger.

The thought all at once made her hot, queasy and a little light-headed. But then she looked at the brave man beside her who'd saved her life, and asked, "What's wrong with you? How can you just calmly be sitting there when you've been shot? Help me get your jacket off so I can see how badly you're hurt."

"I'm fine," he said, wincing while she slipped off his windbreaker. It had been chilly that morning outside the motel, but she'd suspected he'd put it on more to hide his shoulder-holstered gun than because he'd been cold. Beneath the jacket was a shamrock-green T-shirt touting the Santa Clara Lucky Clovers, the right side of which was covered in a dark stain.

Getting a woozy Beau out of the driver's seat and around the front of the car was no easy feat.

Sucking her lower lip, she gingerly raised his shirt over his head to find a bloody mess. But thankfully it looked like the bullet had only grazed him. Nevertheless, his poor, bruised skin resembled a tenderized flank steak.

"How bad is it?" he asked in a scratchy voice.

"If we can manage to prevent it from getting infected long enough to get you to a doctor, odds are you'll survive. Got any bottled water?"

He nodded. "In the back."

"Okay. Looks like the bleeding's long since stopped, so let's get you washed up and laying down on the passenger side. Guzzle that water, and we'll find the nearest town and a doctor."

"W-what about you?"

"What about me? I'm not shot."

"You going to run again?"

"Give me some credit, Beau. You could've been killed protecting me. Yes, more than anything in the world, I want to attend the Culinary Olympics, but not at the cost of someone's life." Especially not his. What he'd done for her might all be in a day's work for him, but…

She was suddenly so overcome with emotion, she couldn't even think, just gaze at him like some dopey starstruck teen. It felt as if only just now had she really, truly seen him. His darkly handsome, whisker-stubbled profile and eyes as deeply brown as the forest around them.

Gracie's mouth went dry.

Marshal Beau was hot.

Marshal-Beau-without-his-shirt was in the realm of ripped Matthew McConaughey!

"Thought you had to pee?" he asked.

"I do. But at the moment, um—" she licked her lips, turning her attention back to his wound instead of his looks "—getting you squared away seems a tad higher on my priority list."

Okay, in her current nurse capacity, seeing how

ogling the patient was highly unethical, she tried
cleaning Beau's wound as quickly as possible with
the few supplies available in the mini first-aid kit
they'd found in the trunk. She'd washed off most of
the blood with water, then daubed at the wound with
disinfectant.

"Damn, woman!" he said with a flinch. "Whose
side are you on?"

"Sorry. This is harder than it looks." The cleaner
she got his wound, the better it looked. Meaning, the
less she worried. Meaning, the more time she had to
peruse his pecs. And his abs? *Oh my...*

She licked her lips.

He smelled good, too. Like mossy, musky woods.
Sweat, leather and dust. U.S. Marshals had been
around a long time. A hundred years earlier, one may
have ridden through this very spot. Gracie had no
problem visualizing Marshal Beau shirtless on the
back of some buck-wild black stallion, gun holstered
low on his hips, a beat-up leather cowboy hat shading
his sexy brown eyes while he forged his way up a
perilous mountain path.

Mmm... If she hadn't been so intent on getting
away from her evil ex and to the Culinary Olympics,
maybe she wouldn't have tried quite so hard to
escape Marshal Beau back when their journey had
first begun.

"Grace? You 'bout done?"

She fell out of her trance to find her fingers had

wandered to his shoulders. Truly yummy shoulders capable of—well, since she was for the moment a medical professional, let's just say they were nice!

"Uh-huh," she said, back to bandaging.

"Good. We should get going. This place gives me the creeps."

"You're not a nature boy?" she teased, packing up the supplies, then handing him three ibuprofens and another water bottle.

He eyed the medicine. Handed it back. "I'm good."

"Take it," she said. "Please. It'll make me feel better."

He shrugged before downing it.

"So what'd nature ever do to you?"

"Nothing. I grew up on the Oregon coast. Me and my sister and two brothers were always outside, but I don't know, I always just feel more at peace in big cities. I like knowing there's life all around me."

"There's life here."

He laughed. "Yeah, bears, mountain lions and those buzzards that've been circling ever since we left the car. They're probably hoping to make me into a bird buffet."

"Oh, they are not," she said with a light swat to those pecs she'd been admiring.

Grinning, Beau covered her hand with his. "Just can't keep your hands off me, huh?"

"In case you hadn't noticed, I was hitting you."

"Uh-huh. Likely story." He winked.

As hot as her cheeks felt, they must be red as the redwood trunk that'd fallen onto the shoulder of the road.

"You ready to go?" she asked.

"Sure," he said. "Hand me the keys."

"I'm driving. You're resting."

"Come on," he complained. "I'm—whoa." He used her arm to brace himself when that first step back into the car had him nearly toppling.

"Less talk out of you," she scolded. "More water *into* you. You're probably dehydrated."

"Yeah, but—"

"You always this lousy at relinquishing control?"

"Yep."

Why didn't that come as a surprise?

Chapter Four

Gracie had wanted to drive back the way they'd come, but just before he fell asleep, Beau—still shirtless, making the drive that much tougher—told her to keep going straight. The dirt road wasn't in that bad shape. Surely it went through to somewhere. Odds were that if they went back, they might have unwanted company.

The gas gauge was on empty, and it was a dicey last few miles until spotting a real live blacktop road. From there, thank God, a small town with a gas station were just a few miles further down yet another twisting mountain road.

Good thing miles earlier she'd peed behind a rock, otherwise, she'd have never made it!

Killing the ignition in front of the station's only two tanks, Gracie's limbs felt quivery with relief.

As if on cue, clouds parted to make way for warm, early afternoon sun.

"Where are we?" her marshal asked, waking only to catch her in the act of helping herself to his wallet.

"Gassing up. Need anything?"

He tried easing upright, and winced. "A new body that doesn't hurt."

"Sorry." And she was. If she hadn't been so stubborn about leaving her car behind to be towed back to Portland, he wouldn't have been shot. "I'm fresh out of bodies, but I can get you some yummy powdered sugar doughnuts." Since the start of her pregnancy, she'd worked hard to eat as healthy as possible, but something about being shot at called for massive doughnut consumption!

He made a face. "Thanks, but I'm well enough to make the trip inside on my own."

"Great. But just in case, you're going to wait for me to help. And you need a shirt, too."

"I thought I was in charge here?" he said with a weak smile. A smile that did wonders for her knotted stomach. He really would be okay.

"What's wrong?"

"Nothing." She swiped at a few silly tears. Jeesh, pregnancy hormones. Made a girl cry over every little—and not-so-little—thing.

His latest groan sounded more like the mental anguish she'd identified during their previous verbal battles. Only this time, she wasn't battling. "What is it with you women? I ask what's wrong, and you say nothing. Yet next argument, first thing you'll throw in my face is how—" He raised his voice to a feminine falsetto. *"I was crying and you just ignored me. Didn't even ask what's wrong."*

Sniffling, she said, "I need to pump the gas."

She'd turned when he shot his hand out to grab her wrist. "Level with me. You're thinking of running again, aren't you?"

"No," she said. "What I'm thinking is that being shot at scared me to death. You nearly dying was…" She shook her head, hating it that again she felt like bawling.

He rolled his eyes. "I've had worse cuts shaving."

"Yeah, well, outside of a few paring knife incidents, that's the worst I've ever seen. And, I don't know…" She flopped her free hand at her side. "Suddenly this all seems much more real. Like before we'd been shot at, it was all just a cat and mouse thing between you and me." There was no one else at the store except for a lone teenage male visible through the window. He stood behind the checkout counter reading a paperback.

For some reason beyond her comprehension, Marshal Beau released her wrist to instead hold her hand. The thoughtful gesture filled her with unexpected peace. His gentle, reassuring squeeze made her feel worse about having tried to escape him.

Holding on tight to her marshal, Gracie said, "If I worked at it hard enough, all this time I thought I could pretend my ex hadn't really killed all those people. I wasn't *really* about to have a baby with only, like, nineteen bucks in checking and no roof over my head when my landlord finds out I can't make this month's rent. If I studied hard enough, practiced enough, I'd go to the CAI competition and win the grand prize and me and my baby girl would live happily ever after." She laughed through messy tears. "That's what I get for reading too many romance novels. After a hundred or so, you start believing everyone has happy endings. You know, that we're somehow entitled. But now that I'm on the verge of being a parent, it's about time I got used to the fact that that just isn't the case."

"What happened to you?" Beau asked, shifting in his seat to get a better look at the once unstoppable hellion who'd now been reduced to a quivering mess of nerves. "A couple minutes ago, you were on fire. Bossing me something fierce. Now, you…I don't know. You just seem defeated. Like you've accepted the fact your ex won, and the rest of your life's in the crapper."

"You think it's not?" she said with a heart wrenching sniffle.

"There are other cooking competitions, right?"

"No. I mean, sure, but not like this one. Other competitions have prizes like pretty crystal bowls and statues, but a hundred grand? Not even close."

"You know, Gracie, if this is just about the

money, I've got a little socked away. We could maybe work out a—"

They both jumped when a horn honked behind them.

Nothing to worry about, though. Just an impatient cowgirl granny behind the wheel of a one-ton Ford hauling a cattle trailer.

"Guess I'd better get to work," Gracie said, releasing Beau's hand to climb out of the car and return to the pump.

"Let me gas up," he said. "You be in charge of snacks."

"But, Beau…" Too late, he was already out of the car, kneeling at her feet. Tying her left sneaker?

"Can't be too careful," he said. When he finished, he took the fuel nozzle from her small hands.

BEAU DROVE THE CAR from the pumps into a parking spot alongside the store, wincing while pulling on a gray T-shirt he'd fished from his duffel bag.

Inside the small, but well-stocked country grocery, he found Gracie weighed down with half the store. Mayo, shaved deli ham, lettuce, tomatoes, whole wheat bread, a bundle of carrots, salt and vinegar potato chips and milk. All of which she then piled into her latest find—a midsize foam cooler. Chuckling, Beau asked, "Think you've got enough?"

"Of what?" She peered at the cooler's contents. "Can you see something I've missed?"

"How about those mini-doughnuts you seem to like?"

"Whew, thanks," she said, hustling around the end of the aisle to grab a sack. "I have been craving those for the last thousand miles."

"Technically we've probably only been about fifty."

"Yeah, but when you can't go much over twenty miles an hour, it feels more like a thousand." She flashed him a gorgeous smile. One that lit her inside and out, giving Beau the sick feeling he was dangerously close to once again falling under a woman's spell.

Hand to his chest, grinning right back at her, he said, "I stand corrected. A thousand miles it is."

"Thank you." For his agreement, he earned another of her hopelessly pretty grins, then, glancing back to her mountain of food, she asked, "You are paying for all this, right?"

"Yeah."

"Great. Just checking." He shook his head in amazement when after she'd gotten the confirmation on who was footing the bill, she dumped her current load on the front counter, then went back for more—this time for stuff like cream, flour, cheeses, butter and spices.

Before she again wandered off to the store's nether regions, Beau asked, "Grab me a couple fried chicken drumsticks and potato wedges from the deli, would you?"

"Sure," she said. "Where are you going?"

"I'll be at the pay phone. The boss likes it when he knows where to find the witness, but my cell's dead."

She nodded. "You should have something more to drink. What do you want?"

"Surprise me."

"'BOUT TIME you called in," Adam said.

Beau shook his head. "What're you doing back in Portland? Thanks for the backup."

"How were we supposed to know where you were? Found your car's transmitter on the side of the road near some speck on the map called Dotted Bluff. Aside from that, you might as well of vanished."

"Tell me about it," Beau said with a groan, leaning against the store's sun-warmed, white cement block wall while relaying the night and morning's events. "Boss around?"

"Yeah."

"Well? Put him on."

While waiting, Beau drummed his fingers on top of the pay phone. From this vantage he had a clear shot of Gracie and her ever-growing mountain of food. Damn, that woman could eat. He couldn't help but stare at her full lips.

Yeah, he knew it was strictly against company policy, but he was starting to like the gal—a lot. He liked her spunk. The way, even now, after she'd finally come to her senses enough to realize she and the baby would be much safer with him than on their own, she was making the best of the situation by working her way through his cash.

"Franks, here. Logue, that you?"

"Yessir."

"Where the hell are you?"

He sighed, gazing out at a fortress of trees. "Best I can tell, sir, the Middle of Nowhere. Vicente's goons led us on quite a little chase. I took a few fast rights that led us out in the boonies."

"But you've got Ms. Sherwood, and she's in one piece, right?"

Well, if you didn't count her obviously whacked mental state which must be the reason for why she was using his company card to buy out the store. She was currently loading up on eggs and yogurt. "Yeah, boss. She's good."

"Excellent. Get her back up here ASAP."

"You hurting?" Gracie asked Beau. He was back behind the wheel, studying a California map.

"No. Why?"

"You're awfully quiet."

"I'm trying to figure out where we are."

She grinned. "Why didn't you say so? The clerk said we're fifteen miles from Bear Lake, where we'll need to head south at the old T-rex slide in front of the abandoned drive-in movie."

He snapped his map flatter. "Those would be directions to San Francisco, darlin'. Portland's the other way."

"Duh," she said around a nibble of a mozzarella cheese stick. "But here's the thing. If I go back, what am I really doing?"

"Ensuring your safety? Not to mention your baby's?" He shot her a look before reaching over her to shove the map in the glove box, then to fasten her seat belt. "Damn, that hurt," he growled.

"I could've done it myself. And you should let me drive."

"Thanks, but no thanks. And what happened to your heartfelt speech about now that you've seen how much danger you're in, you finally get that I'm right about you *not* going to your competition?"

Seeing how her mouth was still full of cheese, she shrugged. Bite swallowed, she said, "Yeah, but then you said I look defeated. And that's not something I ever plan to be. The CAI competition is crammed with people. No way would Vicente be dumb enough to try anything, and even if he did, I'd have you there to protect me. Mmm…" She took another big bite. "This cheese is amazing. Great texture."

"Have you forgotten that we were *just* shot at? I got hit."

"Sure, but you seem fine now."

"What if next time it's you?"

"There won't be a next time, because I have a secret weapon."

"And that would be?"

"You." She flashed him her biggest smile.

Eyes closed, he thumped his head against the seat back.

"No, really," she said. "I've got the perfect plan. You dress up like my assistant. I'm sure we can get you a uniform on site. They have lots of pockets and stuff, so just in case there's the slightest hint of danger, you could hide your gun in there and be ready for—" She bit her lower lip. "Well, you know. You'd be ready for—whatever."

With his thumb and forefinger, he rubbed still closed eyes.

"If you're not down with the uniform—worried it might affect your manly image—we can always ask the judges to allow you to cook in street clothes. It's highly irregular, and just to let you know, they'll probably nix the idea, but if it means that much to you, it's at least worth a shot." She used her eye teeth to open vacuum-packed baby carrots. "You're not talking. Thinking about the plan? Embellishing? Making it a leaner, meaner—"

"Anyone ever told you, you're nuts?"

"It's not me who's the issue, but my baby." Patting her stomach, she said, "To you, this whole thing—my case—is just another day at the office, but Beau, this fiasco is my life. *Our* life," she said with another pat. "I've trained literally years for this competition. I can't sew or sing. I can't—" she waved her hands "—I don't know—paint a bedroom. But I can cook. I cook so well, the *LA Times* food critic called my basil cream sauce orgasmic. This competition isn't just some lark. I've got a real shot at winning. But, Beau—" she put her hand on his thigh "—to do that, I pretty much have to be there, you know?"

Sighing, he said, "I have orders. The boss was clear. He wants you in a Portland safe house—tonight."

"Come on, Marshal Beau." She shifted on the seat to face him. "It's not like I'm not planning on testifying. Trust me, after having been lied to all those years by my ex, I'm a big believer in truth, and truthfully, no one wants Vicente locked up forever more than me. But think about it, even if he's out of the picture, what then? Yeah, I could get a job flipping hotcakes at IHOP, but why, when my every dream is so close for the taking. Vicente has already robbed me of so much, I can't—won't—let him destroy my shot at winning the CAI prize, too."

Beau's only answer was a groan.

"Take me to San Francisco. Give me just these few days. You can surround me with marshals if you want, just please, Beau, do this one thing for me, and then I'll pop myself into seclusion for as long as it takes. It'll be fun even—just baby and me and...all that prize cash."

"And what do I get out of it—except fired from a job I used to love?"

"Well…" She returned to chewing her lower lip. "Remember that orgasmic cream sauce I mentioned earlier? I've still got a ton more practicing to do on my regional variations. If you're the one guarding me, by default, you'd be my official taste tester."

Rolling his eyes, he said, "Default? I take a bullet for you, and I'm a default taste tester?"

"How about Chief Taste Tester? Taste Test Engineer?"

"Wow," he said, voice flat. "Big improvements."

"So then you'll call your boss and plead my case?"

"That talk we had about you being defeated?"

"Yeah?"

"I take it all back. I'm thinking I liked you defeated."

"That's not nice." She popped a mini-doughnut. "Not nice at all."

"You said you want truth." He winked.

She stuck out her tongue.

"I CAN'T BELIEVE YOU have to stop again already," Beau said, turning off the engine at a roadside park.

"I have to pee. Sue me."

He ignored her cheesy smile.

In the bathroom, Gracie hurried with the business portion of the stop—holding her nose against that not-so-aromatic public rest room funk that sometimes sent her stomach roiling—then dallied over holding her hands under warm water, imagining herself in a steaming tub.

Things between Marshal Beau and herself were strictly business, but after what he'd just done for her, convincing his apparent brick wall of a boss to crumble and allow her to go ahead with the competition, she from here on out vowed to worship the man. How many guys took a literal and professional bullet for a woman all in the same day? But maybe the even better question was why?

Granted, Beau had probably sworn some top secret marshal oath to serve and protect, but he didn't know her. What about her specific case had caused him to go out on a limb?

Turning off the water, drying her hands on coarse brown paper towels, she smiled at her wavy reflection in the shatter-proof, polished steel mirror.

Whatever Beau's reasons, thankful didn't come close to the level of gratitude she felt for the man. One thing was for certain, in the days they had together before the competition, she'd feed him like a king.

"You all right in there?" her marshal hollered through the wire mesh rest room door. His strong, masculine voice echoed through the hard-surfaced space.

"Sure. Be right out." Cupping her hands to her belly, she whispered, "Baby, for the first time since this whole mess began, I'm thinking we just might come out all right."

Outside, temporarily blinded by bright sun, Gracie was surprised to find Beau seated on the ground, surrounded by five kids.

"Think you can fix it?" asked a freckle-faced, towheaded boy. He looked about nine.

"Sure," Beau said. "I'll just need a few tools from my trunk." He came back carrying a screwdriver and wrench, then got back to work.

The whole time, she just stood there, face tipped skyward, drinking in warm summer sun that seemed apropos after the earlier storms. In ultrastill air, the pungent, wonderful scent of pines all around them tickled the insides of her nose. In that moment, she couldn't remember the last time she'd felt so at peace. So normal.

Yeah, Vicente's goons were no doubt still out there, but what was important is that they weren't here. And the way her luck was running, she knew they wouldn't show up in San Francisco, either.

After their losing chase, they knew they were outclassed. Which was why she had the peace of mind to stand in early evening sun, a dopey, kid-loving smile on her face while watching Beau fix a boy's bike.

"There you go," he said to the group after a brief speech about not making a habit of talking to strangers. "Ready?" he asked her.

She nodded, wondering where the crazy wish had come from for him to reach out and take her hand? *Crazyville*, that's where it had come from! But she was headed for *Normalville*, so hands tucked safely in her pink sweat suit's pockets, she led the way to the car. Inside, Marshal Beau again helped her with her seat belt, then headed around the car to climb behind the wheel.

"You tired?" he asked.

"Yeah."

"Me, too." He turned on the engine, easing the car from its parking space back onto the highway. Heading south. "The San Francisco safe house my boss is arranging won't be ready until tomorrow. How about we knock off early for tonight, and head the rest of the way in the morning? I'll get word to my crew and they can meet us here. We'll convoy."

"Mmm…" she said, easing her seat back. "Any plan that involves getting out of the car works for me."

Chapter Five

"Nice place," Gracie said with a whistle. "I like your budget better than mine."

While she finished unloading the cooler's contents into a stainless steel fridge, Marshal Beau set the last of her bags just inside the door.

The five star resort where they'd stopped for the night sat on the shore of Clear Lake, California, nestled among ancient bay oaks and redwoods. The scent outside had been pungent and clean. Inside, like starched linens and a hint of eucalyptus that somehow matched the furniture's clean lines and the overall décor's calming ivory and sage tones. Their *room* was more like an apartment, complete with a full kitchen, two bedrooms and baths and a river rock fireplace with a wide, slate hearth perfect for wiling away a chilly night with a pad and pen, dreaming up new spice combinations for hearty soups. Just beyond French doors was a large deck, and beyond that, miles of glassy lake encompassed by violet-shadowed mountains and forest.

"Glad you like it," Beau said.

Gracie slipped off her sneakers, collapsing onto an overstuffed armchair. Her feet and ankles were badly swollen. Probably not a good sign, but it wasn't as if she'd had a choice in the day's activities.

"You look beat," Beau said, taking the chair beside her.

"Thanks. You, too."

"It shows, huh?"

"When you thought I wasn't looking, I caught you wincing. Your side hurting?"

He half laughed. "Only when I sit, stand or breathe. Other than that, I'm good."

"Why don't you take a nap?" she suggested. "I'll make dinner, then, when you get up, you can start your job."

"Huh?" he asked with a good-natured groan. "What job?"

"You already forgot? You're my official Taste Engineer, remember?"

After making a face, he said, "You're not one of those freaky chefs who makes little veggie piles in the middle of the plate and calls it art, are you?"

Eyebrows raised, hands on what was left of her hips, she said, "With an attitude like that, I might not even *let* you taste my cooking. You'll just be tortured by the intoxicating smells. Kind of like being subjected to hours and hours of foreplay without ever getting—" Reddening, she covered her mouth with her hands. "Well, you know what I mean."

He cleared his throat. "Yeah, I, ah, think I get the picture. Only with a sales job like that, I'm thinking why would I want to nap when it sounds like a pretty good show."

She pitched a paprika-colored throw pillow at him, but he easily dodged.

"Hey," he complained with a twinkle in his eyes. "What's the deal with this security team abuse? You're the one who called your cream sauce orgasmic."

"No, if you'd been listening, you'd remember it was the *LA Times* food critic who did that. I was merely his muse."

"Ah, well, glad we cleared that up. If there's one thing I hate, it's an egotistical chef."

"Known many have you? Chefs?"

"Dozens. Each and every one a royal pain in my ass." A slow, devastatingly sexy grin told her he was only messing with her, but it also said a few other things she'd never expected to hear. Stuff like not only was Marshal Beau good to have around in case one of your ex's hit men decided to shoot at you, but it reminded her what a long time it had been since she'd looked at a man and felt a tingle of anything beyond... What? Geesh, Vicente's last stunt had her so messed up, she couldn't even label what it'd ultimately done. Just that she was a mess inside, but that tonight, with no more effort than a little good-natured joshing around, Marshal Beau had yet again made everything all better.

"Judging by those football-shaped feet of yours," he said, "I'm thinking it's you who needs a nap. How about you wow me with your culinary skills tomorrow night? I already told the boss we need to set you up in a safe house that has a great cooking space."

"For real?" That Beau would've thought of such a thing... Her eyes welled.

"Yeah," he said with a slow wink that caused a somersault of excitement in her belly. "If I hadn't thought of you needing to practice then what kind of assistant would I be? That is, assuming I get to perform other duties beyond my already taxing engineering gig?"

"Trust me," she said, pushing to her feet. "You're hired. But there will no rest for the weary. With under a week to go till my only shot at salvation, I've gotta practice."

Crossing the room, she landed on the sofa, then leaned the short space over the sofa's arm to grab the floral tapestry suitcase carrying her recipes. Had she been alone, she'd have hugged the thing. Sure, it would sound stupid to anyone else, but those recipes were quite literally her life.

Gingerly setting it on the coffee table in front of the sofa, she unzipped it all the way around, then flipped the top open to reveal an intricately filed system of thousands of pink index cards containing various concoctions she'd tried from all over the world, such as Lithuanian sauerkraut soup and fried Baltic herring in onion and cream sauce. Some she loved, some were marked with a big, black X, meaning to her own palate anyway, the combinations weren't overly pleasing. The recipes ranged from first course soups and salads to intricate desserts. Many cooking competitions focused on specialties, such as pastry or main courses, but the CAI required a chef be well-rounded in all areas of cooking and food preparation—not relying on the skills of a team, but his or own personal abilities.

Glancing Beau's way, she asked, "Ready for your first assignment?"

"Depends."

"On what?"

"Does it involve leaving this chair?"

"Only your arm. Think you could reach to the side table, pick up the phone and punch in the number for room service?"

"Thought you had to practice?"

"I do. But seeing how we've been blessed with this great setup, I'm going to need a few more supplies. While you were lugging suitcases, I checked out the hotel menu. I'm impressed, and hoping we can buy enough raw materials from the kitchen to put our night to good use. Let's see," she said, snatching a pencil from the suitcase's side pocket, along with a chef's hat-shaped scratch pad. "Sea bass would be super, along with scallions and watercress and—oh, if they have enough to spare, some of those baby…"

Beau groaned. "Woman, anyone ever tell you you're high maintenance?" He planted his hands on the chair's arms and pushed up, but then winced, and eased back down. "Damn."

"Thought you were feeling better?"

"I'm okay."

"Maybe before we do anything about dinner, we should find you a doctor."

"Seriously, Gracie, all I need is a good night's rest. In the morning, the rest of the crew will be here, and if I'm still hurting then, I promise to get it checked out."

"All the same," she said, eyeing him for signs he might be fibbing about the true extent of his pain, "let's have a look." After placing her stack of Argentinean recipe cards on the table, she stood, then motioned for him to do the same.

He did, and when he raised his T-shirt, she sucked in her breath. "My God…" The skin around the bandages and ointment she'd applied was angry red and swollen. She went to him, lifting a corner of one of the bandages. "We've got to get you a doctor. I'm no expert, but I think it's infected." His skin felt feverishly hot.

"I can't believe you," she said, up and already on

her way to the phone sitting on the kitchen counter. She dialed for the front desk, requesting a physician. When the clerk asked what the problem was, she delivered a vague answer about Beau having an infected cut.

"Nice job leaving out the bullet wound part," he said with a slow grin once she hung up.

"Hush. You're probably delirious."

Next, she called room service, ordering two steaks with all the trimmings, along with milk and Sprite. She could practice later. Right now, getting Marshal Beau all better had jumped to the first item on her agenda.

"What if I don't like steak?" he asked.

"Tough."

"I see Bossy Gracie's back."

"She never left."

He shivered. "It's cold in here. Want me to make a fire?"

"It's at least eighty-five in here, and no. I want you to let me help you to bed, then get some rest."

"Hey," he complained while she gingerly tried wrangling him from the chair. "Have you forgotten who's boss here?"

"Not for a second," she said with a sweet smile. "Me."

"MA'AM?" the doctor said. "Would you mind showing me the patient's ID?"

"Sure," Gracie said to the forty-something, impeccably dressed man. He looked straight off the rich people golf course. Cobalt pullover perfectly matching his plaid pants and visor. Vincente had worn similar outfits to his weekly foursome. Seemed like another lifetime since she'd kissed him for luck on his way out the door. The very thought of being within kissing range of the man now made her shudder.

"Ma'am?" the doctor said. "ID?"

"Oh—sorry. Is everything all right? Is Beau going to be okay?"

"If he follows my instructions. How long ago did he receive this injury?"

She had to pause a moment to think. Here, in this serene room, having been shot at seemed like another lifetime, too. "This morning," she said. "We were, um, hiking. He took a nasty fall."

"I know it's a gunshot wound," he said. "Mr. Logue explained he's a marshal, but all the same I'd like to see ID. He says it's in the kitchen, beside the phone."

Gracie found it there, beside the car keys and her purse. That looked odd—seeing her purse beside another man's wallet. It didn't feel right, just handing over something so personal of Beau's to a stranger. Handing over the incriminating evidence she'd found on her ex—now that had been a pleasure.

"All gunshot wounds have to be reported," the doctor said, making notes. Finished, he turned to her. "You all right?"

"As well as can be expected," she said, fumbling

her hands along her bulging tummy. "And room service should be here soon, so that's a good thing."

The smile he cast didn't reach his gray eyes. Apparently they'd not only interrupted his golf game, but he must've been winning. "All the same, with your permission, I'd like to check your blood pressure and those swollen ankles."

"Look, I don't know what Beau told you, but—"

"Let the doc check you out," Beau bellowed from the bedroom.

Rolling her eyes, fifteen minutes later, Gracie was diagnosed with slightly elevated blood pressure and told to stay off her feet as much as possible. Duh. Like she couldn't have figured that out for herself? She seriously needed to practice, but just for tonight, she'd make do with studying her cards.

"I'm leaving a prescription for antibiotics with the Concierge Desk. Someone here at the hotel will have it filled and brought up for Mr. Logue. In the meantime, watch your salt, take your prenatal vitamins and drink plenty of fluids. I'd like for you both to stay here in town for at least one more night. Mr. Logue needs a follow-up visit. Infections like his are nothing to toy with. He should know that."

As abruptly as the doctor had arrived, he left. Yippee. The guy was about as much fun as an empty doughnut bag.

Gracie stuck out her tongue at the closed door.

Creeping into the bedroom, she checked on the patient.

"I'm awake," he said. "You're not very good at being sneaky."

"Gee, thanks." She perched on the edge of the bed, trying not to look at his impressive bare chest. Eyes on his pinched expression, she said, "You look like you're in agony."

"He gave me a shot." He shook his head. "I could take amputation better than a shot."

"Sorry." Scooting further back on the mattress, she asked, "Was it in your butt?"

"No," he said. "Why? You wanna see?"

"Eeuw." She swatted him.

"Ouch. We back to marshal abuse?"

"You'll know when you're being abused," she said with a sassy wink. "Now, you've got antibiotics on the way, but did the doctor give you anything else? Pain pills?"

He nodded toward a white paper packet on the bedside table. "But I'm not taking them."

"Why? You're in pain."

"I'm also on duty," he pointed out, making an awful face as he tried gingerly sitting up in the bed.

Lips pressed tight, she marched into the kitchen for water.

"Hey, where are you going?" her bad patient shouted.

A minute later she returned, holding out the glass. "Here. This might help the medicine go down."

"I already told you—not happening. If I'm out, who's going to make sure you don't escape?"

She laughed. "How stupid would I be to go back to driving myself, paying for myself, staying in crappy roadside motels when I've got you as my new official team sponsor?"

"Good point," he said with a feeble grin. "But what if the opposing team shows up in the middle of the night?"

"Vicente's thugs? Here? Have you already downed a few of these babies?" She reached for the packet, scanned the instructions, then shook one into the palm of her hand. "Says you can have up to two every four to six hours, but in deference to your completely unnecessary suspicions, how about taking just one?"

"Really, Grace, I'd love to, but—"

"Please. I can't stand all your wincing and pinching. Really messes up your handsome mug."

"You think I'm handsome?"

"I wouldn't go that far…" she teased.

A knock sounded on the door.

"Mmm…Dinner." She hopped as efficiently as a very pregnant woman could off the bed. "Don't go anywhere."

Laughing, taking the one pill, he said, "For once, I have no intention of fighting you."

Gracie hustled to the door for some unfathomable

reason actually feeling happy. Just thinking about that steak already had her mouth watering. After all, woman cannot live on donuts alone!

Smile lingering on the corners of her lips, she opened the door for the room service guy who wheeled in their meals on a cart.

"Anywhere special you want these?" the gangly teen asked.

"Just set everything on the counter, please. I'll take care of distribution from there." Apparently he wasn't as thrilled to be here as she was, as he didn't so much as crack a grin at her joke.

Oh well, she thought she was funny.

"Oh—and if you would, please leave me one of your smaller trays. I've got a sickie in bed."

"Yeah, sure."

After taking his time unloading, he held out a small, black leather book and pen. "Sign here, please, and the bill will be added to your room."

"With pleasure," she said, giving him a generous tip to compensate for his having to be at work on such a glorious summer night instead of off making out with his girlfriend.

"Thanks," the kid said, expression much lightened by dollar signs. "Let us know if you need anything else."

"I will," she said, following him to the door. In deference to Beau's goofy fears, after closing it, she locked up tight.

In the kitchen, she tooled around making up the tray for Beau. Hopefully he wasn't yet asleep. She'd like for him to have at least a few bites of steak for when his antibiotics were delivered. They always made her nauseous when she took them on an empty stomach.

Another knock sounded on the door.

Speaking of which... "That was fast," she muttered, shaking her head. This place was amazing. What the employees lacked in demeanor, they made up for in speed.

Unlocking the door, she said, "That was—"

Her next plan of action was to scream, but her ex clamped his hand over her open mouth.

"Ah, darling," he said in his low, elegant voice with its hint of a Bolivian accent. "I'm pleased you're happy to see me. It's been a while since our last time together, and we have much to discuss."

Chapter Six

Beau drifted in and out of a restless sleep.

After caving on Gracie's needling to take a damn pill, as much as it rankled him to admit it, it felt great being able to breathe again without that searing pain in his side. Probably not the brightest of ideas—taking a pill—seeing how he was on the job. But up here in this swanky hotel, he felt safe. Or was that the drug talking? Numbing his usual radar?

"No…you won't do this to me again…."

Live or Memorex?

Remembering the old commercial slogan made him smile.

Beau stretched in the bed. Sure felt good being off duty. The last few days had been intense. Now that Ms. Sherwood was safe, maybe he'd check into taking some of that vacation time he'd been racking up. Head down to her hometown in Georgia. Check on that cute little baby of hers.

While he was down there, he really ought to also check out whatever was making all that racket.

Get away from…

A man was laughing. It wasn't one of his brothers, so who the hell else would be stopping by this time of night?

"Beau! Help!"

He shot up in bed, and it all came rushing back. The cat and mouse game with Gracie. Getting shot. Getting patched up by her. Again, by the doctor.

All was tomb quiet as he reached under his pillow for his .38, then eased out of bed.

Goose bumps sprang up his forearms.

Apprehension or fever chills?

"Gracie?" he hollered. "You all right?"

Nothing.

Had it all been a dream?

Throwing open the bedroom door, he charged into the living area only to feel even worse than when he'd gone to bed.

Gracie's once meticulously arranged pink index cards were scattered to every corner of the room. A crystal lamp lay broken beside an end table.

"Gracie?"

The door leading to the deck was open, the white curtains writhing ghostly in the cool mountain breeze. He ran that way for a quick look, but she wasn't outside.

Back in the living room, he threw open the door, charging into the hall.

The elevator dinged.

"Beau! Pl—"

He took off running but was too late.

Praying whoever had her didn't do their job on the way down, or stop on another floor before reaching the bottom, Beau tore into the stairwell, ignoring the cold slice of the stairs' metal safety strips on the soles of his bare feet.

At the bottom, he prayed he'd beaten the elevator.

But as was generally the case with him, those prayers went unanswered. He bolted into the lobby only to see some slick dude in a suit guiding Gracie pretty as you please right out the front door toward the valet parking attendant.

The drug was making Beau dizzy as hell, and all of the sudden there were two of everyone. Two Gracies. Two dudes in dark suits whose posture told him they more than likely held guns pointed in the smalls of Gracies' backs.

One hand to his forehead, with his other, Beau braced himself against a wall.

Christ, he needed to snap out of it.

"Sir?" a kid dressed in a sissy-ass red bellboy suit asked. "You all right?"

"No," Beau said. "Yes. I mean, get me security. And whatever you do, see those men and women over there?"

The kid gave him a funny look. "I see one man and one woman."

"Right. Whatever. We can't let them leave."

"Security," the kid mouthed into an outdated shoulder mic. "You might wanna hurry. We got a perv down here in the lobby. No shirt or shoes. Sounds drunk or high. I need someone to help me restrain him ASAP."

"No," Beau said. "I'm not the one you want. It's him." He took his .38 from the back pocket of his jeans—where he'd stashed it during his trip down the stairs—and charged toward Gracie's captor.

"Everyone down!" someone shouted. "He's got a gun!"

"Beau!" Gracie screamed.

"Gracie, my love, you're hysterical. Contain yourself." The guy who'd clamped her left arm hauled off and slapped her. Slapped her!

Charging, Beau rammed shoulder first into Suit Dude. "You wanna hit someone, try me."

"With pleasure," he said through gritted teeth, giving Beau a hard right.

"Shoot him, Beau!" Gracie cried. "Just shoot him!"

While Beau reeled from the impact of the guy's a-little-too-impressive blow, a car pulled under the hotel's covered entry.

Suit Dude, yanking Gracie along by her arm, ran that way. "Give me the keys!" he shouted to the valet attendant.

The wide-eyed attendant did as he'd been told, tossing them over the low roof of a red Jaguar.

Suit Dude opened the passenger side door. "Get in," he said to Gracie, "or I'll kill every one of these nice people. Including your boyfriend."

"Security! Freeze!" A rent-a-cop charged Beau from behind, slapping him in cuffs, yanking him back from the curb.

Another rent-a-cop shouted, "You there, in the car, release the woman and step aside with your hands up!"

Suit Dude shoved a screaming, crying Gracie the rest of the way into the car, gave the crowd a calm, over the shoulder smile before firing off a few rounds, then climbed behind the wheel.

"Dammit!" Beau said, bucking to escape the oaf restraining him. "Go after him! Don't you freakin' know who that is? Don't you freakin' know who I am?"

By the time Beau relayed the details of the case, Gracie and her charming ex were long gone.

Adding insult to injury, it started to rain.

"YOU BE A GOOD GIRL," Vicente said, voice low and elegant, barely audible over the driving rain and windshield wipers. They'd been traveling north on the same highway Beau had driven earlier, but were currently stopped for what looked like an accident. Police were going from car to car, having brief conversations with the drivers, then letting them go.

Gracie selfishly prayed the traffic wasn't about a wreck, but her baby and her. It had only been twenty minutes since she'd stupidly gotten in the car with this monster. Could Beau have had time to set up a roadblock? Was she important enough for local police to go to all that trouble? Would they do it to catch Vicente? Not caring what becomes of her, just as long as they caught their man?

"So much as a peep out of you," Vicente said, "and I'll step out of the vehicle and stroll down this line of cars, shooting all the mommies and daddies and babies right through their windows. You wouldn't want that to happen, would you, Gracie Louise?"

She spit on him.

He smacked her across her already throbbing left cheek.

"It doesn't matter if you kill me," she said. "You're done. My testimony is just a technicality. The police have your stupid book."

"Such unpleasant talk during this lovely rain." He switched on a CD player. Soft classical strings barely drowned out her pounding heart. "Were you always this unrefined?"

"Screw you."

"Ah." With the gun still in his right hand, he skimmed it across the crown of her head. "Enjoyed our last time as much as I did, huh?"

"What happened that night—" She shook her head. "You're a sick bastard. We were already divorced."

"I was giving you a gift to remember me by."

"This baby is yours. How can you want to kill your own flesh and blood?"

Just three more cars and it was their turn to talk to police. At much as it agonized Gracie to give voice to the heart-wrenching questions that'd been eating her soul for all these months, if it kept Vicente talking, he wouldn't be shooting.

"Tsk, tsk," he said with a wag of his gun. "Are you trying to make me angry? I told you to never refer to the unborn child as mine. You're a whore. Let's leave it at that."

She spit at him again.

He slapped her again. "Really, Gracie Louise, my patience is wearing most thin. I find the thought of blood on my custom leather upholstery detestable, but make no mistake, I will be done with you right here on the side of the road."

Two more cars.

Vicente switched his gun to his left hand, punching numbers into a dash-mounted cell with his right.

"Yeah, boss?" said a gravelly voice over the car's audio system.

"There's been a slight delay, but I'd like you to remain at the originally planned rendezvous point."

"Yessir."

"Thank you, Marcus. That will be all." Vicente pressed a disconnect button. To her, he said, "Isn't modern technology lovely? I adore gadgets."

Reaching past her, into the glove box, he pulled out a long silver tube. "You don't mind if I smoke?"

She ignored him, keeping her gaze tightly focused on the freedom to be had just on the other side of her window.

One more car.

Rain hammered the roof.

Gracie's heart hammered, making it hard to even breathe. Wonder what that grump of a doctor would say were he to take her blood pressure now? Cloying cigar smoke couldn't help.

Vicente asked, "Do we need to go over my instructions for your behavior when the patrol officer arrives?"

"No," Gracie said between clenched teeth.

"Excellent. Now is not the time for a tantrum."

With a white-knuckled grip on her door handle, Gracie went over her options. Jump. Scream. Wrestle for Vicente's gun. Those were it.

Vicente lightly stepped on the gas, moving the car up in line, then pressing the button for the automatic window. "Good evening, Officer."

Please, Gracie prayed. *Please, let this be a roadblock set up specifically to catch this monster. Please.*

The cop tipped his hat. "Evenin', folks. There's been a landslide up ahead, so you'll want to keep it slow, then do a U-turn about fifty feet up. Only way out tonight is back the way you came."

Jump?

Scream?

Gracie had to do *something.* Now!

"DAMMIT!" Beau raged, kicking the toe of his bare foot against the metal base of the rent-a-cop's desk. "Don't you get it? This woman and her baby are going to be killed. It's not a matter of if, but *when*. Now let me the hell out of these cuffs so I can do my job."

The second security guard stepped into the office and shut the door. "His story checks out, boss."

Beau exhaled the breath it felt like he'd been holding for the past thirty minutes.

Rent-a-Cop One unfastened Beau's cuffs.

"Plus, you're in luck," the guard said while Beau rubbed chaffed wrists. "'Bout an hour ago, there was a big landslide up near Legion. State police caught your guy in the roadblock."

"And Gracie?" Beau asked.

"That the preggers gal?"

Beau snatched the inconsiderate prick by his shirt collar and shoved him against the wall. "To you," he said, teeth clenched, "her name is *Miz* Sherwood."

Leaving the guy gaping, Beau snatched his piece off the desk, then strode back out into the lobby.

Waiting for an elevator, he ignored the gaping stares of other guests scrambling to get away from the crazy guy with no shirt or shoes and a gun.

At the room, thankfully the door was still open. He snatched his keys, T-shirt, wallet and shoes, then left.

Time for a chat with Vicente Delgado.

"WHAT DO YOU MEAN he got away?" Beau asked the officer working the roadblock. The rain had lessened to a cold mist, and small groups sat along a guard-rail, talking quietly, or just staring with hollow eyes. A quick scan showed Gracie wasn't among them. "Do you have any idea how many murders that man is wanted for? Not to mention thirteen bank robberies and a frick-frackin' drug trafficking ring."

"Sorry," the man said. "It's already been a long night, and once the little lady jumped out, screaming for help, then your guy started shooting, things went to hell in a handbasket awfully fast." He pointed down the road, at the at least twenty-car pileup—in front of which was a mountain of still-oozing mud. "Folks realized there was a guy up here with a gun. Next thing we know, they all started flooring it this way. Didn't know about the slide. Just all crammed into each other. Looked like a giant accordion. Shooter took off in my ride. We commandeered another vehicle to chase him—a beater Ford Fairlane. It was the last car in line in the northbound lane. After ten southbound miles, the left front tire blew and your guy was gone."

Beau sighed. Rubbed his eyes with his thumb and forefinger. "And the woman who was with him?" he was almost afraid to ask.

"Oh—she's fine. Ambulance ran her over to the hospital." He whistled. "Don't mind tellin' you, that is one brave little mama."

Relief shimmered through Beau, the force of it

leaning him over to the extent he had to brace his hands on his thighs. "Where's the hospital?"

He got directions, then climbed back in his car, ignoring the gnawing ache in his side, the pounding drug-induced hangover in his head.

If only he hadn't taken that pill. He'd have been hurting, but with a clear head, his reaction time would've been sharp. Who knew how many seconds that damned mental fog had cost. It could've cost Gracie her life—their case against Vicente its best witness.

Beau drove into the night, through inky darkness laced with silvery sheets of rain. Funny, but it wasn't Gracie the witness he was thinking of, but Gracie the woman.

The bossy woman.

The laughing woman.

The woman with a bona fide miracle growing inside her bulging belly and pretty blue eyes and a Southern accent sweet as banana cream pie.

The woman who for some unfathomable reason suddenly meant more to him than any mere witness ever should.

BY THE TIME Beau reached the emergency room, his stomach hurt worse than his side. He was a seasoned, field-tested marshal. He didn't get emotionally involved in his cases. Sure, he cared what happened to the witnesses he was paid to protect, but he didn't get physically ill worrying about them. His heart didn't race and his palms didn't sweat and—there she was, waiting for him on a bench beside the door.

Her dear left eye blackened.

She smiled at him and he lost it, pulling her into his arms. "I'm sorry," he said into her hair. "So damned sorry."

"For what?" she said, voice vibrating warmth across his chest. "You didn't do anything."

"That's right," he said, pushing her gently away so he could punish himself with another look at her face. "I didn't do a goddamned thing to save you."

"That's so not true," she said. "If you hadn't showed up in the lobby when you did, Vicente would've gotten me in his car without anyone being the wiser."

"Yeah, but it was a freak of nature that ultimately saved you. Not me being in that lobby. Hell, by the time the rent-a-cops back at the hotel finally got their heads out of their asses long enough to let me out of those damn cuffs, you were already safe."

She hugged him. "Do we have to go over this now? All I want to do is sleep."

"Sounds good. What do we have to do to get you checked out?"

"Nothing." She beamed up at him, killing him with the sight of her bruised and nearly swollen shut left eye. Thrilling him with the knowledge that she was safe and didn't blame him for her close call, even though there was no one else to blame. "Our favorite doctor showed up. He's adding this bill to your tab."

"Great," Beau said with a quick kiss to her forehead before swooping her into his arms and out into the night.

BACK IN THE NOW trashed hotel room, eyeing the damage done to her precious recipe cards and the serene space where she'd found the first smidgeon of happiness in more months than she cared to remember, a hard knot formed at the back of Gracie's throat.

I'm not going to cry. I'm not going to cry.

Remember? She and her baby now reside in *Normalville*. There was no blubbering there. Women didn't get hauled off by their crazy, murdering ex-husband's there.

Everything was happy.

Sunshine all the time.

Beau stood behind her, quietly shut the door, then stepped around her, sliding the glass door leading to the deck closed, falling to his knees to begin piling the mess wind, rain and Vicente had made of her cards.

The sight of him, a virtual stranger on his knees in an attempt to help her win a stupid cooking contest she probably wouldn't even live long enough to compete in further hardened the knot in her throat, made it tough to breathe.

No crying in *Normalville*.

No crying in…

Hot tears stung her eyes and she clenched her hands so tightly her nails dug into her palms. The events of the past months—*years*—came rushing back. Hitting hot and fast and as unexpected as tonight's summer storm.

Tears started.

Great, racking sobs she was helpless to stop.

Her marshal placed a neatly stacked pile of pink on the coffee table, then went to her, silently pulling her into his arms.

"H-he forced himself on me," she told him. Beau was the only one on the planet she'd ever told. Not her mom, dad, or supposed friends who now wouldn't have anything to do with her. "I—it was the d-day our divorce had become final. H-he just walked into the apartment I'd been staying in near the restaurant, and—" The rest was so horrible, so brutally, morally wrong, even now, more than eight months later, she couldn't bring herself to relive the specifics. "I—I couldn't walk for two days. T-that's how bad he hurt me."

"Let it out," her marshal said into her hair, softly stroking, smoothing, touching her more gently than she'd ever dared believe any man could.

She wasn't sure how long she stood there like that, her hands tucked against Beau's warm, solid chest, his arms wrapped around her.

"I'll kill the bastard," he finally said.

"Before finding out I carried a life inside me, I could've killed him myself."

"And now?"

Chin almost touching her chest, she sighed. "I'm just tired. I don't know what to think other than if I don't get at least twenty hours sleep, I'm going to suffer a major meltdown."

"Hate to be the bearer of bad news," he said, rubbing her shoulders with strong, warm strokes. "But I think you just did."

She laughed through a tail-end sprinkling of tears. "I think you're right."

WHILE GRACIE TOOK a shower, Beau secured the room against any additional uninvited guests. He'd put in a call to his boss, emphasizing the need for backup—ASAP.

For tonight, at least, Gracie and he would be in serious trouble if they needed to get out in case of fire, but anyone trying to get through the wall of furniture barring the door would make a hellacious racket. Way more than enough to alert him to trouble in time to do something about it. Like turn Vicente or one of his thugs into Swiss cheese.

"Your turn." Gracie emerged from the shower wearing a bubble-gum-pink fuzzy robe and matching towel turban.

"Feel better?" Beau asked.

She nodded, flashing him a bright smile.

"Don't," he said, cupping his hand to her bruised cheek.

"Don't what?" she asked, leaning into his touch.

"Pretend you're fine when you're not. That man put you through hell, Gracie. You deserve a little downtime. You don't have to smile for me. You don't even have to talk if you don't feel like it."

"Thanks," she said, her small hand over his, comforting him when he had nothing but his own guilt for troubles. Her eyes turned shiny again. "I—I hardly even know you, yet somehow I feel like I've known you forever."

"I know," he said, taking his hand back, awkwardly tucking it in his jeans pocket. "I mean, I know what you're saying. I feel the same." He looked away, then back up.

What was he doing?

This woman was his job.

He had no business feeling anything but professional detachment for her, yet his heart raced like it hadn't since his first high school crush.

"So look," he said. "I've been hammering out logistics, and even though there are two rooms, I'm thinking I'll take the sofa—just in case."

She shook her head. "Bad plan."

"Why's that?"

"Why can't you be with me?" She reddened—at least her right cheek that was still a healthy pink instead of black and blue. "You know, just sleep with me."

He couldn't resist raising an eyebrow and casting her a slow grin.

She gave him one of her playful swats. "You know exactly what I mean, Beauregard Logue. After what just happened, I'd feel safest with you beside me. I know it's not conventional, but just for tonight, do you think it'd be all right?"

Now he was the one near tears. God, he was glad she was okay. That her bastard of an ex hadn't hurt her. "Yeah," he said. "That'd be great. Just let me hop in the shower and I'll meet you there."

At one-seventeen by the glowing red numbers on the hotel-provided alarm clock, Beau slipped into bed beside a woman he was so attracted to, he had no business even standing beside her, let alone sleeping with her.

"Beau?" she said in her adorable Southern twang.

"Uh-huh?"

"We never did have that steak."

"Tell me about it. I'm starving."

"Me, too. And this little darlin' inside is really letting me know she's displeased."

While Beau had no doubts Gracie would love a boy all the same, it had been infinitely more kind of the fates to gift her with a girl who would hopefully bear no resemblance to her monstrous father.

"Feel," she said, taking his hand, guiding it to her

belly, granting him access to her wondrous human show. The baby moved its foot in a gentle, one hundred and eighty degree arc.

"Wow," he said. "You weren't kidding. So what happened to the dinner we ordered?"

"I guess it's still on the counter where I left it. But after it's sat out all night, I don't think we should eat it."

"We'll probably be all right," he said.

"Probably?" She laughed. "After all we've been through in the past twenty-four hours, call me crazy, but I'm not in the mood for food poisoning. More like nice, dull predictability. And hot fudge. Gallons and gallons of hot fudge. And vermicelli with chorizo. And garlic butter sautéed shrimp. And ooh—I could seriously go for some *kjottkaker.*"

"Huh?"

"Norwegian meatballs—but if they don't have those, I'll make do with whatever version the hotel kitchen has around."

Shaking his head, he said, "You call in the order and I'll start moving the Great Wall of Furniture."

Chapter Seven

"Where'd you crash?" Adam asked at six in the morning. He was busy checking out the suite of rooms—except for the bedroom Gracie was still snoring in. Beau hadn't had the heart to wake her.

"What's it any business of yours where I slept?"

"Just curious," Adam said, opening the fridge and sticking his head in. "Hot damn. Shrimp and spaghetti? Big brother, I like your style."

"That stuff's Gracie's. I had steak."

"Gracie?" He raised his eyebrows. "Got any left?"

"Huh?"

"Steak?" Adam said. "Any leftovers?"

"No. And get back to the first part of that statement. You implying something? 'Cause if you are, we can take it outside where I'll remind you—"

"Boys, boys, simmer down." Gracie wandered out of the bedroom dressed in her pink robe, slippers and a mess of curls the size of New Jersey. Aside from her black eye, never had Beau seen her look more pretty. "Hi, I'm Gracie," she said to Adam, extending her hand. "We briefly met in Fort Mackenzie. Sorry I had to drag you all the way down here."

"Not a problem," Adam said after reintroducing himself. "And for the record, I'm Beau's bro."

"*Little* bro," Beau was quick to point out. Though Adam hadn't looked at another woman since Angela, to Beau's way of thinking, he was grinning a little too broadly at Gracie for this early in the morning.

But then why should Beau care?

He swiped his fingers through his hair. Gracie was his job. Nothing more.

"Ms. Sherwood," Beau said, "how about ordering breakfast? I'm, ah, going to check on the other members of the team. Adam? You got things under control up here?"

"Roger dodger," Adam said with a cocky salute of his loaded shrimp cocktail fork. Shrimp cocktail. Gracie had had a fit when her fancy schmancy food order hadn't arrived quite per her exacting demands.

Clearing her throat, Gracie said, "After the cardboard that arrived via room service last night, how about I cook breakfast. Crepes, maybe. And muffins with an apricot fruit spread. Marshal Beau, sweetie, think you could find me some cream cheese and fresh apricots?" Index finger to her lips, she said, "I'm pretty sure I got flour yesterday while we were still on the road, but I'm going to need a few other items, as well. Why don't you hold on for a sec, and I'll jot down a list."

"Ms. Sherwood..." Beau clamped his lips and counted to ten. "By this afternoon, we'll be at the safe house. I'll have someone on the team fill your list there. Until then, would it kill you to kick back, watch a little *Price Is Right* and eat normal eggs and toast?"

She pouted. "Could I at least have sourdough bread and fresh orange marmalade?"

Glancing at Gracie, Adam advised, "Don't back down so fast. Those crepes and muffins sounded good."

"Adam," Beau said. "Stay out of it."

"Yeah, but when's the last time we had anything home-cooked, that actually—"

"Adam! Room service. Eggs. Bacon. Toast. *Now.*"

"Yes, sir," Adam said with a generous side of sarcasm.

Gracie stuck out her tongue, after which, his traitorous brother slapped her a high five.

Shaking his head in disbelief, Beau turned his back on them both. Only when he was out in the hall did he indulge in the decadent release of a long-held breath.

What was happening to him?

Seeing Adam hamming it up with Gracie just now hurt worse than the hole in his side. His sudden bout of grumps hadn't been about Gracie's outrageous food demands, but the way she and Adam instantly hit it off.

Where was her loyalty? Had the night they'd just

shared meant nothing to her? Had she forgotten the way he woke, spooning her, with his hand cupping her pregnant belly?

For as long as he could remember, Beau had felt as if he was searching for something always just beyond his reach. For whatever reason, maybe because growing up, he'd spent so much time taking care of his kid brother, Adam, and sister, Gillian, he'd grown to like caring for people. Anticipating needs. Funny, how even though he realized the fact about himself, he still somehow always seemed to end up with career-driven women who didn't need a thing.

Ingrid had been a defense attorney he'd met working a drug case three years earlier. The woman had been insatiable in bed. And at first, hell, he hadn't had a problem filling her every need. But after a while, crazy as it had sounded the few times he'd tried explaining it to one of his brothers, freaky hot sex in passing wasn't enough.

As weeks and months wound on, he'd felt like one of those weepy wives on afternoon talk shows, whining about their husbands spending too much time at the office and not enough with them.

Beau had always considered himself somewhat of a workaholic. He loved his job, but to Ingrid, her job came before all else.

Most nights, she wasn't home before nine, then she'd be gone again by eight the next morning. Most weekends, she'd spent holed up in strategy sessions. And then, she'd stopped coming home altogether. When Beau had accused her of having an affair, she'd denied it. But by that point, it didn't much matter either way. He was no more in love with her than she'd been with him. They'd been a diversion for each other. Not much else. But then she'd announced she was pregnant. And for a while things had changed.

Both of them spent more time at home, together. Talking about the future of their son. Sharing hopes and dreams. But then, just about the time anticipation for his son's birth felt like a living, breathing thing inside him, Ingrid had ripped out his soul with the coolly delivered news that the baby wasn't his after all, but that of one of her partners.

Their divorce had been fast and efficient. Kind of like Ingrid, herself.

But where did that leave Beau? Yet again on his own. No wife. No kid. Not much of anything really, other than work.

He'd told himself he wasn't torn up about his marriage ending, just disappointed. Wondering if it had been Ingrid who had been the problem, or if there had been something he could've done different to make it work.

And then there was Gracie. No doubt he felt overly protective of her pregnancy. How fondly he remembered those few good months with Ingrid during the prime of her pregnancy. And it had been a while since any of his base needs had been satisfactorily met. So sure, spooning with Gracie was bound to wreak bodily havoc.

But bottom line—it hadn't been cool. At least as far as his job description was concerned.

But personally, as a man, Beau hadn't felt that good since before things had gone bad with his ex. Even worse—he'd woken with a raging hard-on.

One he was now experiencing anew.

Dammit, what was he going to do? Not just about the problem in his frick-frackin' jeans, but the sudden tightening in his chest whenever he so much as thought about what had almost happened to Gracie on his watch. And then there were the never-ending what-ifs.

What if Vicente tried grabbing her again? What if at this supposedly safe cooking competition of hers, he tried something really squirrelly, like blowing up the whole damn hotel? The guy was certifiable. There was no telling what stunt he might pull. He was a one man storm, with Gracie caught in the eye.

"YOU DIGGING my brother as much as he's obviously digging you?"

Even though Adam was Beau's brother—especially because Adam was Beau's brother—his feelings, or hers, were not topics Gracie wanted to explore. "Want anything from room service?" she asked, assuming the best plan of action was an altogether avoidance of the subject.

"Waffles would be good," Adam said. "With bacon—and sausage. And what the hell, maybe ham. And hash browns. And plenty of OJ. That's it. I'm still full from the grub we had on the plane."

"Okay," she said, making note of his lengthy order on the notepad beside the phone.

"Why didn't you just fly to San Francisco?" he asked.

"I'm too far along in my pregnancy."

"Cool," Adam said with a nod. "I mean, not that you might pop on a plane, but that—well, you know."

"Sure," she said, wishing the man would just go commune with the fridge instead of studying her like she was an exotic new animal species.

"He's not allowed to like you," Adam said. "That's the only reason I brought it up. The fact that Beau has the hots for you makes for an all-around bad situation. When a marshal falls for a witness he's trying to protect—trust me, I know."

"I'm sure. And trust me, your brother's no more interested in me than he is in going dress shopping at the nearest mall."

Adam downed another shrimp. "He would be."

"What?"

"Into dress shopping if he was buying that dress for you."

"I don't mean to be rude," she said, picking up the phone, "but I'd really rather not discuss this with you—or anyone. Nothing personal, you understand. Just that I think this entire subject is ridiculous."

"Whatever." He ran his finger around the edge of the fluted shrimp cocktail cup. "But for the record, I think you two make a cute couple." He winked. "In case you hadn't guessed, I like food. Lots. Having a chef in the family would be awesome."

Laughing, shaking her head at the improbability of her and Beau ever being more than friends, she abided by Beau's wishes, and called in a room service order. She added a ham and Swiss cheese omelet for herself and scrambled eggs with cheddar, bacon and hash browns for Beau because that's what he'd said he loved to eat for breakfast last night while they'd shared their snack.

And then they'd shared so much more. A brief, but utterly relaxing night's sleep like the kind she hadn't had since school. Since before meeting Vicente.

All night Beau had been such a gentleman. Just holding her. Never even trying to take it further.

After a night like that, spent cuddling and crying and sharing her deepest secrets, how could he now be back to calling her Ms. Sherwood, as if they were no more than casual acquaintances? Did he truly feel that way—like it was all business between them? Or was this new tough-guy act for Adam?

One thing was for certain, along with the items on her grocery list, she wanted to know what made Beau tick.

"I'VE MISSED YOU," Gracie said late that morning in a rare moment alone with Beau. The San Francisco safe house wasn't yet ready because of an electronics problem, so it had been determined the best option was to stay put in their current hotel until all the work was done.

Beau stood in front of the fridge, bracing one arm on the open door. The light cast his face in dark shadows made darker by lack of sleep.

"What time did you get up?"

He shrugged. "I'm thinking it was sixish when Adam and the rest of the guys got here. You were up not ten minutes later."

"I know, but we didn't get to bed till after three. Why don't you take a nap? I did, and I feel much better."

He shot her a look. "I'm on duty. I can't just break for naptime."

He grabbed a Coke from the top shelf, popped the top and took a long swig. After closing the fridge door, not so much as glancing her way, he said, "Well, see ya."

"Where're you going?"

"The elevator. I'll send Adam back in to keep an eye on you."

"I don't want him."

"Why not? I thought you two hit it off?"

"We did. I mean, he's nice and all, but…I want you."

He sighed. "Gracie, look, I—"

"Please tell me what happened to change things between us? Don't get me wrong, I'm not implying we had anything—you know—going on. But I thought we were at least friends. Now… It's like you're upset with me about something. Like you can't even bring yourself to look at me."

"Yeah." Lips pressed tight, he stared at his drink. "Things have changed."

"Was it something I did? Said?"

He laughed, only far from being happy, it was a sad, strangled sound. "Let's just say I got too close to the cookie jar and the boss slapped my hand."

"You didn't do anything inappropriate," Gracie said. "If anything, I'm to blame for whatever might've happened that was a little, well, unorthodox. Want me to talk to him?"

"No," he said, landing a light thump to the wall with the heel of his hand. "God, no."

She cupped her fingers to his shoulder, drinking in his sinewy-hard strength. Her baby's bulge rubbed his back. "What can I do to turn back the clock? Make things the way they used to be between us? I miss you." *I need you.*

"Nothing," he said with another unreadable laugh. "Not a frick-frackin' thing."

WHILE ADAM finished packing Gracie and her eight thousand suitcases for the short hop to San Francisco, Beau slipped out in the hall to call his sister. She and Gracie must be psychic twins as Gracie had her eight thousand boxes and Gillian had left no less than eight thousand messages on his cell.

"It's about time you got back to me," Gillian said, picking up on the second ring.

"Sorry. I've been kind of busy."

"I heard."

"What's that supposed to mean?" Beau said over the barking in the background that he assumed was his niece's golden lab, Barney.

"Give me that! Beau, you'll have to hold on a sec while I—"

The phone went dead.

Beau shook his head. Never a dull moment with his sister and brother-in-law. They had so many kids and pets, Beau wasn't sure how they kept track of them all. Beau for sure wanted a kid—maybe even two. But that was it. Any more, and how did you keep them all straight?

His cell rang.

He glanced at the caller ID, flipped it open. Ugh. "Hey, Gil. What happened?"

"Sorry. Joe got a new parrot and Barney wants to eat it, so I got him a little parrot squeezie toy, but Meggie's got a stuffed animal that looks just like it, and Barney thinks that one's his, but—"

"Gil, I hate to cut you short, but we're shoving off in a few minutes. Is there a reason you called?"

"Duh. Adam says Gracie Sherwood's a looker."

"And…"

"That you two didn't just spend last night to-gether—in the same bed, but the night before that, as well. Care to comment?"

"No."

"Is it true she's a world-famous chef?"

"Yes."

"So back to the bed thing, Beau, what were you thinking?"

"It was for safety's sake, all right? The first night, I had to cuff her to me to keep her from running. And the second night…"

"Barney! Give me that right—Beau, I'll call you back. And when I do, you'd better be prepared to spill details."

The instant his sister hung up, Beau turned off his phone. He'd have to remember to give the dog a new rawhide come Christmas, because he'd certainly earned it.

As for the second night he and Gracie had slept together, Beau hadn't deciphered it for himself yet. How was he supposed to explain it to his nosy sister?

TRAVELING SOUTH on I-5, in the center of a marshal caravan of black SUVs, Beau glanced Gracie's way. Dressed in yet another a pink jogging suit, with her curls piled high, she sat cross-legged on the roomy passenger seat, one by one, picking tiny candy dots off a sheet of wax paper. She'd selected the snack from the hotel gift shop after having declared she couldn't survive without something sweet. And after the hardships she'd been forced to thus far endure, the least Beau could do is buy her candy.

He'd seen the look Adam shot him after he'd given in to her latest demand, but had chosen to ignore it— the look, not the demand. Poor Gracie. After what she'd been through, what was the harm in providing her with one of life's little luxuries?

What's the harm? His conscience all but screamed. The harm was that he was becoming attached to her.

No. He tightened his grip on the wheel. She was a sweet, smart, brave woman he greatly respected. Period. The fact that they'd ended up in bed together, so to speak, well, that was inconsequential. The fact that he'd very much liked being in bed with her, nothing more than Mother Nature doing her thing.

"When I was alone with Adam," she said out of the blue, "he said a couple things I thought were odd."

"Like what?"

"For starters, he thinks you *like* me." She winked. He growled.

"But then he said you're technically not allowed to like me, and that if you did, he knew from experience falling for a woman you were sworn to protect was a bad idea."

"And…"

"I was just wondering…" She angled on her seat to face him, unintentionally haloing her crazy curls in the afternoon sun. Her poor, battered cheek was now green, and dammit, he could deny it all he wanted, but yeah, he did feel strongly toward Gracie. Even more so after hearing the depth of what that bastard ex of hers had put her through. "What happened? Did your brother have a forbidden fling?"

"I wish that'd been the extent of it," Beau said with a sad laugh. "This goes back a long way. Adam had only been in the service for a year or two. He got assigned to protect a judge's daughter who'd been receiving death threats. She was hot—really hot. College coed still living in her sorority house. Adam hadn't been out of school all that long himself. For him, it was like old home week, only now he had this shiny silver star and a gun to help raise his social status—not that he'd ever needed help, but you know what I'm saying. The chemistry between him and this girl was electric. You could see how much they were into each other, and man—" he rubbed his jaw "—that kind of stuff is taboo. Just not good for business."

"So what happened?" Gracie asked, fingering a long curl.

Sighing, gazing off at the approaching urban sprawl of San Francisco, he said, "Whoever came up with the phrase *loose cannon* must've had my brother in mind. There's never been a direction the kid could follow. First, he and this girl played around. It was a relatively harmless flirtation. But then we'd catch them sneaking off to dark corners. The attic of her sorority house. The basement of his old frat. She was miked for sound, and their make-out sessions got *waaaay* out of hand. I told him, 'Kid, you gotta get yourself reassigned. Not only for your own good, but hers.'" Beau shook his head. "He didn't listen. Secretly went out and bought her an engagement ring. Then they start sleeping together. He got himself pulled from the case after that. Put on probation. During which, he took the opportunity to help Angela move out of the sorority and into his apartment—where he was convinced he could keep her even safer."

"What'd her dad say about all this?"

Beau laughed. "Everyone adores Adam. The kid's a charmer. Like a big, lovable hound. The judge had come from a poor background, worked his way through college on scholarship. He fell in love with the idea of his daughter falling for a *real* man as much as his daughter fell for Adam. They'd even started planning their wedding when—" He stopped. Shook his head. Even now, thinking about it teared him up.

"Oh, no…" Gracie's slowly rose her fingers to her mouth. "His gentle warning was about him thinking you're falling for me and I'm going to die."

"Bingo."

"But I'm not going to die," she said with far less

conviction than Beau would've liked. "And we're not lovers. Just friends."

"Right."

"So really, the both of us will from here on out be the very models of professionalism, right?"

"Hell, yeah. Strictly by the book."

"COME ON, Marshal Beau! I dare you! Just one jump!"

From Gracie's vantage on top of the bed, his objections to her jumping seemed so small as to not even exist. Normal, that's what this was. Jumping on motel beds was a pleasure she hadn't indulged in since she'd been ten. Only just now, did she realize how much she'd missed it. Only the apartment Uncle Sam had put her up in wasn't a motel, but a glitzy, gold-toned, five-thousand-square-foot, vanilla potpourri-scented masterpiece that according to Adam had been confiscated to pay back taxes from an actor he wasn't at liberty to name. Whoever the guy had been, he had fabulous taste—gaudy, but fab!

The master bedroom she'd been given was bigger than her whole apartment back in Fort McKenzie, and the bed had been custom-built to fit the turret of the nineteenth-century Knob Hill mansion. Like an elegant circus tent, heavy gold and ivory brocade fabric draped the ceiling and walls. Deep gold satins and velvets covered the bed Gracie couldn't wait to nap in—right after she finished organizing her recipe cards and got that shopping list to Adam.

"Quit it," Beau said, presumably in regard to her continued jumping. His grumpy tone said he was trying to sound mean, but he couldn't quite hide the grin tugging corners of his gorgeous lips. "I mean it. You're going to go into premature labor, and then what kind of trouble will we be in?"

"I'm fine," she said, giggly and out of breath.

"I'm not."

"What's the matter—besides your crappy mood?"

"There's nothing in that rule book we're supposedly following that covers what to do if the very pregnant woman you've sworn to protect starts jumping."

"Oh—okay," she said, carefully walking to where he stood scowling at the foot of the bed. "But you have to get me down from here." She held out her arms and, fool that he was, he stepped into them, allowing her to snuggle them around his neck, wrapping him in her sugar-sexy smell. He tucked his hands around her, lingering a little longer than necessary when she rested her head on his shoulder, her warm breath puffing clouds of what-if on his neck.

"Mmm… That was fun," she said. "Thanks for the ride."

"Sure." What if he hadn't been assigned to protect her? If they'd met at the park or grocery store or a coffee house or through mutual friends? Would his life still be this upside down?

He supposed he could let her go just anytime, but why, when she felt so damned good? Her womanly curves pressed against him, flooding him with warm glimpses into a future that would never— must never—be.

"I still say you should have a turn, though." She slipped down in his arms until her words heated his chest. "Because I'm getting the idea that you, Marshal Beau, aren't real big on having fun."

"Since when are you?" he asked, fighting the urge to kiss the tip of her cute nose.

"I don't know." She left his hold to spin in a small, little girl-type circle, tilting her head, all that crazy hair of hers streaming down her back. God, what he would give to kiss her throat. Cup his hands around her breasts. Neither of which would be professional, but at least he was honest. "I guess since being with you, for the first time in I don't remember when, I feel safe enough to be silly."

"Have you forgotten what just happened with your ex? I couldn't have screwed the pooch much worse on that one."

"No," she said with a firm shake of her head. "Stop blaming yourself. If anyone's to blame, it's me. I shouldn't have nagged you into taking that pain pill. I shouldn't have blindly opened the door. I should've let those people in the lobby take their chances while I took mine by running into your arms. The whole night, Beau—it was a mistake. At least up until the point when we finally got back to the hotel, then fell asleep in each other's—well…" She looked down and shyly smiled. "You know what I mean. Ever since then, I've felt truly safe. Invincible."

"No one's truly safe." He tucked his fingers under her chin. "You know that, don't you? I mean, not even the president. If Vicente wants you bad enough, Gracie, he *will* get you."

"Gee, Mary Sunshine, thanks so much for the encouraging words." She turned her back on him, playing with a remote that caused a mammoth flat screen TV to rise from a low, gilded chest designed to look like a dresser near the foot of the bed.

"Aw, I didn't mean it like that and you know it. It's just that—"

"What, Beau? What do you want me to say? That I feel wretched around you? You should take it as a compliment I don't."

"I do," he said, gently nudging her to make room for him to sit beside her. "But what I don't want is you feeling a false sense of security. Two sets of eyes are better than one. You'll be even safer now that you've got a whole team, but that doesn't mean you're suddenly bulletproof."

She rolled her eyes.

"Seriously…" Hand on her chin, he forced her to meet his stare. "Be careful."

"Can we please just drop it?" she asked, backing away from him to press her index fingers to her temples. "Forgive me if I needed a little fun. From now on, I'll do my best to keep it strictly business."

She flicked on the TV, found one of her favorite cooking shows, but then switched to somber news about the Middle East. "Wouldn't want any entertainment going on in this room."

"Knock it off," he said. "You know what I mean."

Of course she did. But she wasn't about to let him know. Another thing she wouldn't let him know was that she suddenly felt foolish for spending time on frivolous things like bed jumping when she should've been studying or—

"Come on." He took her left hand, pulling her up in the bed.

"Where are we going?"

He half grinned. "That's for me to know and you to find out."

Chapter Eight

Hands on her hips, Gracie suspiciously eyed the orange and yellow oversized swing set nestled deep within an indescribably lush rooftop garden, complete with an ornamental koi pool. The sweet smell of so many flowers she couldn't begin to name them all was dizzying. The sight of big, strong Marshal Beau standing in an apple tree's shade, looking so proud for having presented her with fun, far better than acres of flowers. Up here, high atop the city, or for that matter, the world, even knowing three other marshals lurked somewhere nearby didn't dampen her mood. For here in this paradise, Beau by her side, Gracie felt a million miles from trouble.

"Get on," he said, hand on the small of her back, leading her down a winding brick path to the swings. "I'll push."

"I don't know..."

"Why not?"

"Those seats aren't big enough for me and my new and improved derriere."

"They're plenty big," he said with a sexy-slow grin. He plopped her onto the nearest of the two, and she fit just fine. What wasn't fine was the rush of hot awareness strumming through her every time he was near—let alone touching her! "Hold on," he said, "and I'll give you a ride."

"All the way to the sun?"

"If that's where you want to go. Just know if you're that far out of my sight, once I get you back, I'd have to cuff you again."

"Mmm…" she said, loving the feel of soaring through a secret garden, soft summer heat mingling with the moist scents of freshly watered plants and cypress mulch.

Eyes closed, smiling, she breathed deeply, forever capturing the place, the scent, the feel of Beau's strong hands on her back.

Each time she came in for a landing, he sent her higher, whether he knew it or not, further instilling the feeling that with him, she was safe. It might only be an illusion, but up here, protected by lush foliage and sky, she seriously doubted her ex was going to jump out from behind a potted hibiscus, guns blazing.

And if he did?

What a way to go.

Suddenly, melancholy washed over her. "That's enough. Please help me stop."

"Why? We've barely been out here five minutes."

"Come here," she said. He gave her a funny look while she stood, pointing at the swing's wide, black vinyl seat.

"You want me to swing?"

She nodded.

"Marshals don't—"

"Do it, or I'll run again."

He groaned, shot her one of his famous put-out-with-her looks, then did her bidding. "I'm sitting. Now what?"

Eyeing the fittings holding the swing in place, she prayed they were solid, then sat squarely on Beau's lap.

"What the? Gracie, we can't—"

"Just relax. It's no fun swinging alone, and seeing how there's no way you can sit on my lap, I thought this might work."

She glanced over her shoulder just in time to catch him rolling his eyes.

"Oh, quit being such an old fuddy duddy," she complained. "You're turning out to be the very antithesis of fun."

"And you're turning out to be a major pain in my—"

She shifted just far enough to kiss him.

Nothing major.

Just an innocent press of her lips to his. And if the rockets zinging through her reflected more than that actually having happened?

Well, she was sorry.

Not really, she thought, kissing him again with a smile. But she supposed in all fairness to Beau, she should be.

"What'd you do that for?" he asked, eyes darting all around.

"No biggee," she said. "Remember back when we were getting shot at, and I was in that panic, and instead of the requisite slap, you kissed me?"

"Yeah," he said with a funny sideways nod. "But that was business."

"So was this. You needed a kiss-slap to remind you to lighten up. That we're just friends who—"

His cell rang.

And rang.

And rang.

"Don't you need to get that?"

"Definitely no."

Now he was kissing her. Only it wasn't a simple, chaste, professional, *emergency* kiss, but an exquisite study in pressure. Heady, wondrous pressure that eventually led to a mesmerizing sweeping of tongues.

She again shifted on his lap, slipping her left hand off the swing to the playground of his hair. Her right fingers, she clenched around the swing's chain where Beau's joined hers. He stroked her back, sending her contentedness level spiking off any known charts.

"Damn," he said when they parted for air. "Who knew swinging was this much fun?"

"I didn't mean for that to happen," she said. "Sorry."

"I should be," he said, gazing up at the clear, blue sky. "But I'm not."

"It was just a kiss," she said. "Friends kiss, right? Like at office Christmas parties and stuff?"

He chuckled. "You try laying a *friendly* kiss like that on any one of the guys I work with, and you'd have to be locked up for only my pleasure, and they'd have to be tortured to a slow, agonizing death."

"My, I wouldn't want any of that to happen," she teased, batting her eyelashes. "From now on, I vow to never kiss your *friends*—only you."

"That'd be great," he said, clenching his jaw. "Aside from one nagging thing."

"And that would be?"

"I think you know. It has a little something to do with me getting fired, and you not being wholly protected if my mind's on making out with you instead of guarding you."

Sadly she nodded.

With his feet braced on the sand beneath them, he wrapped both tree trunks he called arms solidly around her, resting his head on her right shoulder, exhaling his warm breath on her neck.

And then he was standing, taking her along for the ride. Once he'd planted her feet safely on the ground in front of him, he clamped his big, rough hands to her cheeks. "Seriously," he said, perilously close to her lips, "as great as that was, it can't—won't—happen again."

He released her and she just stood there, feeling deeply alone and a little—no, a lot—silly for ever having kissed him in the first place.

"Hey," he said, back to touching her with his finger under her chin. "Where'd my smile go? And anyway, Adam's probably back by now with your grocery list. Shouldn't you be practicing?"

Unbelievable. The man tells her they shouldn't be kissing, then had the nerve to call her smile *his*? Though Gracie would've loved nothing better than to tell him off nine ways to Sunday, what was the point? They weren't dating. After this week, once they got back to Portland, he probably wouldn't even be assigned to her, meaning she'd never see him again. So why did she even care if he casually flirted? Why did she care if he seemed to be touching her or brushing against her as much as humanly possible?

Why did she care? Truthfully, because she liked his flirting and touching and most especially, his kissing. Which was too bad, seeing how not only did he have a job to do, but so did she. She was in San Francisco not to kiss, but secure a future for herself and her baby. Every ounce of her mind, body and soul must be focused on the CAI competition—not Marshal Beau.

Which was why, after indulging in one last lingering look at his disgustingly handsome mug, she left him to head inside.

"Where you off to in such a hurry?" he asked, chasing after her.

"Like you so politely pointed out, I should be practicing cooking—not seduction."

Grabbing her upper arm, he pulled her to a stop. "Am I wrong in sensing a tone?"

"No tone," she said, refusing to meet his direct stare.

"Hey…" His voice was surprisingly soft as he gave a quick visual sweep of their perimeter. What? Was he checking if anyone else was witnessing their tiff? "What I said back there…I never meant to hurt your feelings. I just—hell. I'll say it. I'm into you, but I'm seriously not allowed to be. So there. It's out on the table."

Swallowing hard, she nodded. Somehow, it had been easier denying her own attraction for him when she'd still been upset. Now, she didn't know what she felt, other than majorly confused.

EARLY THAT EVENING, Beau stood guard in the kitchen that, according to Gracie, was like a chef's Disneyland. Stainless steel appliances sat amongst coffee-colored marble counters and ornately carved dark wood cabinets. Tying in with the gold prevalent in the rest of the apartment were golden canisters and plates and knickknacks that individually, no doubt cost more than a couple months of his pay. But as physically nice as everything in the kitchen was, nothing was more beautiful than Gracie. She was decked out in chef's white, clearly in her element as she bossed Adam, making him fetch flour or chop green peppers.

At the start of what had turned into a marathon cooking session, Beau would've bet big money his little brother would run screaming within fifteen minutes, but apparently, Adam, as well as every other marshal assigned to this case, was smitten—not just with Gracie, but also her heavenly food. None of the foreign-sounding recipe names made any sense, but the tastes varied from smooth and creamy to hot and spicy to sinfully rich.

If there was one thing Adam loved, it was food. And seeing how in addition to being Gracie's gofer, he was also her taste tester, he wasn't about to make way for someone else to get his job. Beau had pointed out a couple different times that it was supposed to have been *his* job to test Gracie's creations, but neither she nor Adam seemed to have heard his complaints.

Not that it mattered, seeing how every marshal present got to taste most everything, but it was the point of the thing. Gracie had promised Beau the job. Trouble was, it wasn't so much the job he wanted, but the chance to be close to her. To brush up against her on the way to the fridge, or while landing a pot on the stove. To kiss her sweat-dampened nape where tendrils of her piled-high curls threatened to spill.

Like it or not, he was a goner.

Oh, he could try denying his attraction to her. He could tell himself their kiss had just been playing around. But the truth was that he'd been on this job for nearly a dozen years and never once had he come close to kissing a woman he'd been sworn to protect.

Hell—he'd never even wanted to kiss one of them.

He exhaled a sharp breath, rubbed his aching forehead.

The ethical thing to do would be assign Gracie to someone else. Take himself completely off her case.

It sounded good in theory, but that was the problem with theory. Didn't allow a whole lot of wiggle room for those troublesome gray areas.

For the most part, he was doing an okay job.

Okay?

While Gracie got uncomfortably close to Adam in the process of showing him how to sliver almonds, Beau silently snorted. Okay wasn't good enough for protecting a woman's life. Especially a pregnant woman's life.

So what was he supposed to do about it?

His loyalty should be to the job. The ideal of protecting the witness against all who may bring her harm. And so would he now be lumped into that category? Of bringing her harm?

That supposedly causal garden kiss wasn't a good

thing. And those half-dozen calls he'd ignored from his sister? That wasn't good, either.

Oh, hell yeah, that kiss had felt awesome—but morally, it had been wrong. As much as it sickened Beau even thinking it, he had to make a solemn vow never to kiss—or even think about kissing—Gracie again.

"DID YOU REMEMBER to take your antibiotic?" Gracie asked Beau from her seat across from him at the ten-foot marble slab dining room table. He was officially off duty for the night, meaning she'd wrangled him into eating with her, so she didn't have to sit in the cavernous room alone.

"Yes, ma'am." He took another bite of Maine lobster chowder with coconut, corn and lemongrass, closed his eyes and swallowed. "Good Lord, this is good. Those judges would be insane not to pick you as the best chef ever."

Being reminded of the contest stole her appetite— as did seeing one of Beau's fellow agents peek into the room from his station out in the hall. With just the competition, so much was at stake. Then there was wondering if Vicente would be there, trying to kill her while she whipped up a caramel soufflé…

Her throat tightened and eyes welled.

While she was casually hanging with Beau, or cooking, focused on creating the most insanely delicious dishes ever, she didn't think about why all these hulking men were around. Adam was just Adam, a funny, perpetually hungry guy who was turning out to be a great assistant. And Beau was—she didn't even want to think about what Beau was to her.

Definitely more than friend.

She'd seen the flash of hurt in his eyes when she'd asked Adam to help her instead of him, but he had to have known why. That it would be too hard for her to concentrate on cooking with him so near. With her so aware of his every move and masculine scents instead of those of her dishes.

Dropping his fork, he asked, "You okay?"

"Sure," she said with a start. "Just dandy."

For a few agonizingly awkward moments, he eyed her, then took another bite and leisurely chewed. After a sip of iced tea, he asked, "I ever tell you about my family?"

This was obviously his bumbling man attempt at switching the subject to something safer than her melancholy mood. But seeing how she didn't have much else to do, and her feet throbbed from way too much time spent pacing the kitchen, she said, "I know you have another brother and a sister, but aside from that, nope. You've been pretty closed mouthed."

After his next bite, he said, "Along with my sister, Gillian, comes an eccentric-as-hell brother-in-law. His name's Joe. Then there's big brother Caleb, and his new wife Allie. They have a little boy—Cal. Joe and my sis have his little girl from a first marriage and a toddler, Chrissy. Then there's my dad. Mom died." A muscle in his jaw twitched.

"I'm sorry," Gracie said, wanting more than anything to reach across the table to give his hand a comforting squeeze. Judging by his suddenly dark expression, she assumed his mother's passing must have been a fairly recent thing. But that afternoon, somewhere between her fourth batch of caribe honey glaze and second of aioli sauce, she'd come to the realization that he was right about the two of them keeping it cool. They both had their work to focus on. More importantly, she'd already made a disastrous choice in one man, why take another chance? On the surface, Beau seemed like everything she'd ever wanted in a guy, but then so had Vicente. "Are you still having a tough time?"

"With what?"

She nearly choked on her latest sip of decaf iced tea. "Beau? What do you think? Your mom."

"Mom died years ago. Back when I was a kid. Yeah, it sucked bad at the time, but I've made peace with it."

"Then why do you all of the sudden seem as down as me?"

"Family. I was just going to point out how lucky you are not having them constantly in your business. I've ignored about eighteen calls from my sister since this morning."

"Why so many?"

"No doubt Adam opened his big mouth and got her suspicious."

"About what?"

He gave her a look.

"Us?" she squeaked.

The set of his mouth was grim.

"But there is no *us*," she pointed out.

"That's what I told my sister the first time she called, but apparently she wasn't happy with that answer. She's got this serious problem in that ever since she and Joe hooked up, she wants everyone else to live the same fairy tale they do." He snorted. "Ever since my divorce, I've tried—"

"You're divorced, too?"

"Yeah. I never mentioned it?"

"Um, no. But then you're not the world's most talkative guy, so it's not a big surprise I know next to nothing about you."

"Like I know all that much about you?"

She rolled her eyes. "Correct me if I'm wrong, but don't you have a file containing everything about me from the color of my hair and eyes to what I wear to bed?"

Gracie wouldn't have thought it possible, but Marshal Beau actually blushed.

Grinning, sipping more tea, he said, "That last fact's, ah, one I had to learn from experience. How about filling me in on the rest?"

"What do you want to know?"

"*Everything.*" He reached for her hand, but pulled back. Instead, busying himself with his fork.

"That covers an awful lot of ground."

He met her stare. "I'm up for the trip. You?"

Chapter Nine

During the past couple hours, Beau repeatedly told himself professional courtesy was the only thing keeping him glued to the conversation. It was what he told himself when he asked Gracie what her best Christmas gift ever was—a dollhouse her grandparents made. And why she had a penchant for wearing pink—because it was soft and soothing and made her forget the harshness of recent circumstances.

They'd moved from the dining room to the kitchen where he'd washed up while she insisted on making a batch of the most insanely delicious brownies he'd ever tasted. And now, they were back in the rooftop garden, sharing a covered, bench-style swing nestled in a fragrant tangle of night-blooming jasmine.

The only drawback to the moment was that Beau wanted to kiss her. Bad. Inside, their conversation had been relatively private, but outside, even though the swing was isolated, three of the marshals on duty lurked nearby.

"Mmm…" Gracie said, resting her head on his shoulder, only conflicting him more as to how he could feel such attraction for a woman he barely knew. "It's so beautiful up here, I hate to go in, but it's probably getting late."

"You have to practice more tomorrow?"

"Uh-huh. Thursday I'll be in press conferences all day, which only leaves four days to perfect my repertoire."

"Explain to me again how this thing works."

Beau's cell rang.

"Hold that thought," he said, checking to see who it was, only to find his sister's number. He turned off the damned nuisance.

"Who was it?" Gracie asked.

"No one important. Go on, get back to telling me about your competition." He'd much rather hear that than a lecture on what would no doubt be the evils of him hitting it off with an assignment when Gillian had pretty much done the same thing with her husband, Joe.

"Ever seen *Iron Chef* on Food Network?"

He frowned. "Sorry. I'm more an ESPN kind of guy."

"No apologies necessary," she said with a big grin. "On the show, two big name chefs battle it out in a TV kitchen. They're assigned a main ingredient—

say squid or tofu. From there, they have an hour to create as many dishes possible showcasing the required ingredient. Different courses are always appreciated by the judges. Anyway, the CAI competition runs pretty much the same, only we're asked to showcase countries. The more regional specialties I can squeeze in the better."

"Who decides which country you land? I mean USA would be a no-brainer, but what if you get Mongolia?"

She laughed. "Each round's competing chefs draw cool little wooden cutouts of the countries from a giant globe. You only have three seconds to draw—so no memorizing edges to cheat. And actually, you'd be amazed by some of the yummy foods that come from Mongolia. It gets a bad culinary rap."

"Okay, Miz Smarty Pants—wow me with something from Mongolia I wouldn't yack up."

"For starters," she said with a teasing smile that lit her eyes, even in the dim garden light, "there's the perennial favorite, *huushuur.* Or, in civilian terms—fried meat pasties."

"Yum." Nudging her shoulder, he said, "Sounds pornographic."

The comment earned him a swat. "Okay, if you don't like that, how about a nice *marmot boodog?*"

"Huh?"

"All you do is take a freshly killed marmot, remove the innards, fill the empty cavity with hot stones, then tie it up. The heated stones cook the meat. For browning, you'd traditionally put it over an open fire. Voila—*marmot boodog*."

Beau blanched. "Would your feelings be terribly hurt if I just sat on the sidelines during your competition? Munching on some nice, safe popcorn?"

"Not a problem," she said with a laugh. "Although I'm thinking for practice tomorrow, instead of all those relatively tame dishes you all had today, I'll step it up a notch with something exotic. Maybe Balinese."

"Sign me up—assuming you'll be wearing a coconut bra and sarong."

Laughing, she asked, "That sounds hot—only where's the baby going to fit?"

"Oh, yeah." Scratching the stubble shadowing his jaw, he said, "Funny, I don't even think of you as pregnant—not that you being pregnant is a bad thing—more like really cool, but—" Grinning, shaking his head, he said, "You know what I mean."

"Yeah…" She took his hand for an all-too-quick squeeze. "I do. And thanks. When you've been walking around with a wreck of a body like mine, it's nice to know a fine specimen of the opposite sex finds you attractive."

Preening, snatching back her hand to kiss the palm, he said, "You think I'm a fine specimen of manhood, huh?"

"Definitely. Grade A, prime meat."

"Good to know," he said, splaying her fingers only to interlock them with his. Lord, she felt good. All warm and soft, but at the same time, strong. Strong enough to pull off a win at this competition. Strong enough not only to survive after what her ex had done, but also to thrive. "You look pretty," he said, voice husky with unidentifiable emotion. From the jasmine growing beside the swing, he pinched off a blossom, tucking it behind her left ear.

"I—I thought we weren't going to do this," she said, lips parting. She touched the tip of her tongue to her upper lip, looking so unwittingly sexy Beau had to shift in his seat so as not to embarrass himself with the sudden increase in the size of his buttoned fly.

"We're not," he said, going in for a kiss, but not completing the mission. Just hovering, breathing her in, tasting her chocolate-laced breath on his own.

"Is it wrong for me to want to kiss you?" she asked. "Because I do."

"Yeah…" he said. "Know the feeling." Unable to bear not touching her, he landed his hands on the safest spot on her lush little body—the baby. The wondrous mound of life so similar to the one he'd once called his own.

Like Ingrid, Gracie's baby wasn't Beau's, but with Gracie, he found himself not caring who the father was, just that when the time came for the child to enter the world, that he'd be allowed to be there.

A mere inch from kissing Gracie senseless, from breaking his every Marshal's Service vow, he said, "What the hell kind of spell have you put me under?"

"It was the brownies," she said. "They work every time."

"Oh," he teased, taking her again by her hand, twining their fingers, stroking her palm with his thumb. "So this is a wile you use often to trap poor, defenseless marshals?"

"Hey, no one's trapping you," she teased with a sexy wink. "You're free anytime to leave—you just don't get to take any brownies with you."

"In that case," he said, "I'm afraid you're stuck with me for quite a—"

"Ah-hmm." Mulgrave busted in on their private world, his thoughts on Beau's lack of professionalism fairly evident in the grim set of his mouth. "Beau, could I have a word, please."

Feeling like he'd just been doused with cold water, Beau released Gracie's hand and stood. "You be all right for a second?"

"Um, actually," she said, licking her lips, her gaze darting from Beau to Mulgrave and back, "I think I'll just turn in for the night."

"'Night, Ms. Sherwood," Mulgrave said.

She cast him a faint smile before slipping off into the garden, heading down the path leading for the rooftop door.

Once she was out of earshot, Mulgrave said, "What the hell do you think you're doing?"

"If you'll excuse me," Beau said, "I've got paperwork to fill out before turning in."

"Look," Beau's old friend said, "Adam told me there was chemistry between you and our latest client, but I didn't believe him. I said, no way. Beau's a consummate professional. But, jeez, man. You were all over the woman."

Beau hardened his jaw. "We done?"

"No, we're not. I've just got a couple reminders for you. First, not so long ago you nearly got yourself killed over this woman. Two, you nearly got her killed by falling asleep on the job back in Clear Lake."

"Thanks. I needed reminding."

"Glad to help," Mulgrave said, not looking glad, but furious. "Snap out of it. Gracie's a sweet, cute woman, but she's a job, man."

"I know, but…"

"*What?* What possible excuse are you going to spout to condone your behavior?"

Beau started to speak but then clamped his lips tight. How would he even begin explaining his mixed-up feelings where Gracie was concerned? Part of the attraction had to be related to how badly he wanted kids of his own. Granted, he and Gracie shared chemistry, but it had to be more than just that leading his insane urge to be with her—no matter if the price was as steep as his career.

"Well?" Mulgrave goaded. "Let's hear it. What's your excuse? In her current state, it's not like she's a sex kitten, so why?"

"Couldn't tell you. There is no excuse." After a deep breath and long exhalation, Beau said, "Thanks for the heads-up. You're a good friend." Patting Mulgrave's shoulder, Beau headed down the same path as Gracie, determined more than ever to head straight for his room, as opposed to hers.

"RISE AND SHINE, sleepyhead."

Hot damn, Beau thought, rolling over in his bed. Was he really being sweetly lured awake by a woman's sexy voice and the scent of something warm and cheesy?

"Come on, handsome. I already covered for you once, but I don't think that grouchy boss guy will buy it again."

Huh?

Beau eked one eye open to find blond—and curls. Lots of them attached to one of the prettiest, sun-flooded faces he'd ever seen. After washing his face with his hands, he opened both eyes to peer into the gorgeous blue eyes of the one thing he wanted, yet couldn't have.

Gracie Sherwood.

Against the backdrop of what the guys had affectionately dubbed the beach room because of its pale blue walls and giant palm-fringed beach mural, she held out a plate for him. It was loaded with an awesome smelling cheesy egg concoction, canta-loupe and watermelon balls and a blueberry muffin that if he'd had to guess, he suspected she'd been up early making from scratch. "Hungry?"

"Yeah, but you didn't have to go to all this trouble." Edging up in the bed, he said, "As pregnant as you are, I should be bringing meals to you."

"Agreed," she said with a gorgeous grin, "but seeing how I need to be cooking every spare second of every day, it really doesn't make much sense for me to lounge in bed while you cook and wait on me, does it?"

"No," he said, making room for her beside him, then patting the bed. "But then it doesn't make sense for you to be serving me, either."

"Oh—it's okay," she said. "I told your boss you're still under the weather from your gunshot wound. He gave you the day off."

"My *boss?*" Taking the plate from Gracie and digging in, Beau asked, "Franks is here?"

"I don't know about Franks, but some grumpy guy named Caleb showed up around five—just when I'd finished a batch of trout balls."

Beau shuddered.

"Not a fan of trout?"

"Or my big brother."

"That frown with legs is the same Caleb as your brother?"

"Unfortunately. Usually he's an all right guy. The only time he's angst ridden is when an assignment isn't going his way."

"Everything's fine here," she said, appearing

dumbfounded as to what could be the reason for Caleb's sudden appearance. "For being on lockdown, I'm having a great time."

"Yeah, well…" After nearly choking on his latest bite, Beau tried finding the right words to tell her she wasn't supposed to be having a great time, but a safe time. The last thing he, or any other of the marshals assigned to protect her, was there for was to entertain her. In fact, most assignments—

A harsh knock sounded on the closed bedroom door. "Beau? You decent?"

"Crap," Beau growled under his breath. Here he was in bed yet again with Ms. Sherwood. Only making matters worse was the fact that she was now happily munching melon she'd snatched off his plate and he had no shirt or pants on. Thank God for the boxers he'd worn to sleep in.

Before waiting for Beau to answer, Caleb barged right in. "Ms. Sherwood. Sorry. I didn't know you were in here."

Liar.

"It's all right," she said. "We were just sharing a bite to eat."

"Yes, well…" Caleb cleared his throat. "You see, Beau's not really supposed to be fraternizing with you. It's a company policy kind of thing. You understand."

"Um, sure," she said, shooting Beau a pained look before gingerly shoving up from the bed and onto her feet. "Sorry. Didn't mean to cause waves."

"You didn't," Caleb said with what Beau recognized as his best PR smile. His older brother was aiming to be the next presidentially appointed U.S. Marshal of Oregon, and so he made a federal case out of following rules—except when they applied to him.

Once Gracie had left, closing the door behind her, Beau said, "Does the name Allie ring a bell?"

"Don't go there," Caleb growled.

Beau laughed. "Give me one good reason why I shouldn't. You gonna stand there and deny things went a little awry on that mission? Or that you never once held her hand or laughed or shared a meal or God forbid kissed her until *after* you were officially off her case?"

"Dammit, Beau," Caleb said, thumping the nearest wall. "Don't you dare bring Allie into this. We were almost married. She had my son."

Beau set his plate to the bedside table and stood. "So that makes everything you did all right?"

"For the record," Caleb said, finger pointed at Beau's chest, "Allie and I never slept together while I was on duty."

"And you think Gracie and I have?"

"I know you have."

"And given my long history of womanizing, you think me incapable of *just* sleeping with a woman. Holding her till she feels safe?"

"Jeez, Beau," Caleb said with an angry slash of his hand through his hair. "I don't know what to think, only that both Adam and Mulgrave have found you in compromising positions with Ms. Sherwood and while I haven't told Franks yet, you know he wouldn't like it. Vicente Delgado's case is ultrahigh profile. I'm shocked Franks is even letting Ms. Sherwood go through with this whole cooking thing, but I guess he has his reasons."

"Um, yeah," Beau said, grabbing his plate, then heading for the door. "Ever heard of a little thing called public opinion? If sweet little pregnant, star witness Gracie had run off and vanished, or worse yet, gotten hurt while running, do you think the DA would've been happy?"

"Oh, so in essentially playing house with her all these days, you've just been doing your part to keep her safe until her slimeball ex goes to trial?"

"Damn straight."

Caleb sharply laughed. "Just keep deluding yourself, little brother."

"You want me off?" Beau said, sick of feeling guilty over the best thing to have happened to him in years. "Fine. I quit."

"Oh, stop. Even when you were a kid you had a flair for being dramatic."

"And you had a flair for being a know-it-all ass."

While Beau stood toe to toe with his brother, a few heartbeats from punching him out, a knock sounded on the door.

"FYI," Adam said, "Gracie just took some New

Delhi casserole thing from the oven. Smells pretty— whoa. Something happen here I missed?" Stepping into the room, he shut the door. Eyeing Beau's plate, he said, "Looks like you're busy. How about letting me unload those eggs for you."

Beau handed him the plate.

Adam dug in. "Damn, this is good. Is there anything that woman can't cook? Seriously, Beau, if you decide you don't want her, I'd be happy to make her my own."

"Stow it," Caleb said to Adam.

"Finally," Beau said with a snort. "Something we agree on."

"Don't be hatin'," Adam said around a huge mouthful of muffin. "What's wrong here that a little good food can't fix?"

"Your brother just quit the service over a woman he's barely known five days."

"You what?" Adam clanged the fork to Beau's plate.

Reaching into the front pocket of the jeans he'd worn last night and flung over a chair, Beau fished out his badge and handed it to Caleb. "You wanted it, you got it."

"Take a deep breath, loverboy. I never said I wanted your star. Just that you need to do a little more thinking with your pants on than off."

Argh! With all his might, Beau shoved Caleb into the wall. "Knock it off. Gracie and I haven't done the deed. We're *just* friends—something that under her circumstances, she could use a helluva lot more of."

"So just like that, you're prepared to give up a career you've worked your whole life for?"

Beau shrugged. "Looks that way."

Adam whistled. "Way to go, man. I've gotta say that if I had it to do over again, I'd have left the service and taken Angela with me—somewhere far away where she'd have never been found."

"You know," Beau said, tugging on his jeans. "That's not a half-bad idea."

"Would you get a grip," Caleb said, shoving him down on the bed. "You barely know this woman. She's damn near eight months pregnant. It's no family secret things ended badly between you and Ingrid—through no fault of your own. And while I'm sure it feels great that this adorable pregnant woman needs you, in a month, just like Ingrid, she won't. She'll pop out her baby—not yours. She'll send the little tyke to day care, then get on with her career, just like your ex. What you feel for Gracie isn't real. It's hyped up emotions brought on by danger and love you still have for a son or daughter who just wasn't meant to be."

Beau shot his older brother a go-to-hell look.

"I know this is the last thing you want to be hearing," Caleb said, "but if you do resign from the service, don't think for a second you're just going to sit around here, living the high life with your new girl. You'll be gone, Beau. And as far as I'm concerned—"

Another knock sounded on the door, then Gillian

marched in. "What's going on? I heard you yelling clear down the hall."

"Beau just handed over his star. He's leaving the service for Gracie Sherwood."

"Oh, he is not," Gillian said. "And you," she said to Caleb, "quit being such a big old grouch and learn the fine art of compromise. Allie said you've been having a lot of heartburn. Is it still bothering you? Because if so, you really ought to go have it checked so—"

The door opened again, this time, without the benefit of a knock. "Hey, guys," Allie, Caleb's wife, said with a friendly wave. "What's up?"

"Great." Beau groaned. "The whole gang's here."

"Damn," Gillian's husband, Joe, said, popping open the door to join the party. He stepped right in, a cookie held to his mouth. "Have any of you tried these Jamaican Boscobel Bear things? I'm not sure who the woman is in the kitchen, but man, can she cook."

Chapter Ten

"You must be Gracie," Beau's sister, Gillian, said fifteen minutes later, pulling her into an awkward hug. "You poor thing. Being pregnant is hard enough without getting shot at."

Beau stood to the rear of the kitchen and let the forces otherwise known as the women of his family take over. For the moment, Caleb had refused to take his star—probably a good thing, seeing how just up and quitting had been rash. But what else was he supposed to do? He couldn't help feeling the way he did about Gracie. No matter how hard he'd tried, the affection for her, the caring, wouldn't go away.

For safety's sake, his family's arrival was a grown-ups only mission, but from where he stood, that would be plenty of folks to ensure a complete mess! Thank God his dad and Allie's mom were back in Portland watching over their wild pack of grandkids.

"Look at all that pretty hair," his sister-in-law Allie

said, helping herself to a handful of Gracie's abundant curls.

Thanks to the bottomless wells entrepreneurial Joe called pockets, they'd all flown via private jet to San Francisco. Seeing how Gillian was still in the marshal's service part time, she said she was there to help further protect their assignment, as were Allie and Joe, but Beau knew better. They were there for one, sole reason—to snoop.

While at one end of the kitchen the ladies *oohed* and cooed over Gracie and her big belly, the men talked security in the library.

Beau wandered that way, despite all that was on his mind, still marveling at the room's at least fifteen-foot tall mahogany-paneled walls and bookshelves loaded with rare, leather-bound, first-edition books. Wood floors were covered in oriental carpets that made his footfalls silent as he approached the group. When the heavy golden curtains were open, the view of the bay was spec-freakin'-tacular. The room's current view of his scowling big brother was less than stellar.

Caleb eyed him and said, "You know you're playing with fire, don't you?"

"Give it a rest."

Caleb crossed his arms and sighed.

Joe asked, "Anyone up for a game of pool? I saw a table in the next room over."

"Sounds good to me," Adam said. "And hey,

let's grab a few more of those Jamaican cookies for the road."

"I'm with you," Joe said, leading Adam from the room.

"I want you off this case," Caleb said. "So does Dad."

"I'm a big boy, Caleb. I can take care of myself. I don't need the whole damn family voting on every little thing I do."

"Your getting shot the other day wasn't a *little* thing. Wise up. You could've been killed. Hell, for all I know, you've still got what happened with Ingrid on your mind. I know it can't be easy, being up close and personal with another pregnant woman. But, dude, Gracie's baby isn't any more yours than Ingrid's is."

"I should blacken both your eyes for that."

"Maybe so, but you've gotta know I wouldn't have said it if deep down I didn't love you enough to not want to lose you. Dammit, Beau, from what I've seen of her, Gracie's a great gal, but is she worth losing your life? I don't get why you're breaking all the rules on this case. What the hell kind of spell does she have over you?"

"*Spell?*" Beau laughed. "Come on, now you're the one losing it."

"Then why did you push so hard for her to go through with this competition? Yeah, we can prob-bably protect her, but the only even marginal guarantee of true safety would be for us to take her back to a Portland area safe house until Vicente's trial."

"She has a lot at stake," Beau said. "A win could ensure her and her baby's future."

"Swell. What does that have to do with you?"

Everything, Beau wanted to scream, but deep down, some of what Caleb was saying was starting to make sense. But how come if he hardly knew Gracie, he felt as if he'd known her forever? How come everything about her from her sweet smell to the feel of her in his arms felt right? Like she'd been there all the time?

"Hot damn!" Joe called from the adjoining room where he and Adam played pool. "I so got you on that one."

"Just wait till my turn," Adam said. "You'll cry like a second-grade girl."

Beau sighed. Squared his shoulders and stared his know-it-all brother head on. "You wanna know why we're going to all this trouble for Gracie? Because that's the way she wants it. If we don't do it her way, I'm telling you, she'll run. And trust me, as the one who had to catch her the last time, it's something I don't ever again want to do."

"So cuff her and haul her back to Portland. Plant a tracking device in her purse and let her run. I still fail to see why there's this need for lack of protocol on your part."

"And I fail to see why it's any of your business."

"Guys?" Gillian touched their shoulders. "Why don't you table this topic and mosey on into the dining room. Gracie's prepared us all an amazing brunch."

"This isn't over," Caleb said under his breath.

"There a problem?" Gillian asked.

"Yeah," Caleb said. "Our brother's a fool."

"Stow it," Beau fought back. "It's not like you didn't pull a few strings with Allie. And what about Little Miss Island Hopper, here? Think she didn't shoot protocol all to hell with Joe?"

"Hey—keep me and Joe out of this," she said. "And, Beau, I think all Caleb's trying to do is gently remind you how much is at stake here."

"You think I don't know?" Beau said, out of earshot but within sight of the table where Gracie sat laughing with Allie and Joe. "Look at her. She's beautiful and oblivious. Even after what she went through with her ex, I still don't think she wants to believe this isn't a game. That her life really is in danger."

"And so let me guess," Caleb said with a huge chunk of sarcasm. "You've appointed yourself her protector? So she can mosey along her merry way, pretending she's on a big adventure? Or maybe reality TV? And don't think Adam and the rest of the crew haven't noticed the way things are between you two. You've fallen for her—hard."

"You wanna take this outside," Beau asked Caleb, fists clenched. "'Cause I've had just about all the family togetherne—"

"Whoa." Gillian stepped between the two brothers. "Caleb, Beau's a professional. Give him some credit. He's following the book as best he can. And Beau, cut Caleb some slack. He's just worried about you—we all are."

"Beau, hon?" Gracie stood beside him, cupping her small, warm hand to his arm. What he wouldn't give to be alone with her right about now. Just the two of them. Sharing one of her unforgettable meals. Talking. Laughing. "Your Belizean breadfruit rolls are getting cold and I also made a mango papaya chutney that I don't think will make you *yack*." Grinning up at him over their shared joke, she winked.

"Thanks," he said, smiling down at her. Lord, she was pretty. Just one look into her blue eyes he could almost forget his buttinski brother even existed. "Let's eat."

With Beau at the opposite end of the table from them, Gillian leaned in to Caleb, whispering behind her hand, "Adam was right. You see the way he looks at her?"

"Kind of hard to miss," Caleb said with a snort.

"What're we going to do?"

"From where I'm standing, doesn't look like there's much any of us can do."

"Maybe Joe and I could talk to her? Offer her a loan so that she doesn't even have to go through with the competition. Once Beau gets home, surely he'll come to his senses and realize it's the thrill of being

out on the road with a pretty girl that has his hormones ramped up."

"Maybe," Caleb said, scratching his head. "Shoot,
I don't know.

"Well, let's both think real hard. Maybe by the time
we finish eating we'll have come up with something."

"PLEASE, GRACIE," Gillian said midway through the
meal. "Forgive me for being nosy, but—"

"You're not nosy," Gracie said in her honeyed drawl.

"Thanks," Gillian said, "but that's not what my
brothers or dad tell me."

Everyone shared a laugh. Everyone save for
Adam, who was still working his way through a pile
of butter-coated Belizean Johnny cakes.

"Anyway," Gillian continued, "you seem like a
real sweetheart, and as such, I'm wondering why
you'd want to put yourself through such a grueling
competition with the added pressure of your ex still
being at large?"

Toying with the three champagne grapes still on
her plate, Gracie said, "Ever since this mess with
Vicente first started, my life has been a shipwreck.
Awful publicity and accusations of me also being
involved in Vicente's filthy dealings forced the restaurant I'd worked years to make a success into
closing. In the neighborhood where we'd lived for
five years and made what I thought were a lot of
good friends, women I'd lunched with and attended

baby showers with, wouldn't even take my calls."
She paused to brush away tears that broke Beau's
heart.

Why was his sister forcing her to hash over all this
again? Couldn't she see Gracie was in pain? "Sis,"
he said, "cut her some slack. It's been a long few
days, and I'm sure she doesn't—"

"It's all right," Gracie said, hand on his thigh. "Let
me finish. It's probably good for me to get all this out."

Gillian and Allie gave her sympathetic nods.

"I've been living—if you could even call it that—
like a pariah. And then when I—I got pregnan…"
She abruptly pushed her chair back from the table,
running for the nearest exit.

"Nice," Beau said, pushing his chair back, as well.
"Way to go at making her feel about as welcome in our
family as a six-headed snake." Giving all assembled
his most disgusted look, Beau stormed after Gracie.

Gillian pressed her napkin to her lips. "Is it just
me, or did he really just imply that Gracie was part
of our family? As if they were married, or at the very
least a serious item?"

"Now, do you see why I called you all?" Adam
said, only just then looking up from his feast.

"SWEETIE…" Beau said in the sumptuous, gold-
plated and marble master bath. The circular tub was
big enough for four, and marble pillars and mirrors
gave the feel of an emperor's pleasure den, only

making it that much more of an unlikely spot for a pregnant, girl-next-door-beauty like Gracie to sob her way into his arms. "You going to be okay?"

Even though she nodded against his chest, he had his doubts. "I—I just didn't want your family to know—about how I g-got pregnant. I—I didn't want them to think ill of me. I—I know they already don't like me, because they think I'm putting you and Adam and all of the other marshals assigned to protect me in danger because of insisting on going through with the competition, but now that Vicente's gone, we're fine, aren't we, Beau? Everything's normal, right?"

"Absolutely." He reached behind him to the counter for a tissue, wiped all around her pretty eyes, being extra tender around her still healing bruise. "And once you start your contest, you'll cook up such a storm those other chefs will weep."

Clinging to him, again she nodded against his chest. "Thank you," she said.

"For what?" *Lousing up an otherwise nice day by saddling you with my family?*

"Just being you. Keeping me safe. I know—better than I know my own name—that as long as I'm with you, Vicente can never hurt me again. You won't let him."

All that whipped cream Beau had added to the four different fruit dishes Gracie had served curdled in his gut.

Christ. They'd been over this. How no one could ever be a hundred percent assured of their safety. Not even the president—certainly not her. Sad truth was, if someone wanted you dead bad enough, they could damn well do the job.

So what now? How did he gently remind her of this? Especially as every day, they grew closer to the eye of the storm. With her as exposed as she'd be at the competition, Vicente was just nuts enough to attack. If all went well, if he so much as tried looking at her, all marshals assembled would take him down. And if things didn't go well?

Swallowing hard, clutching Gracie still closer, Beau refused to think about it.

"I'M SORRY if my wife's drill sergeant routine got you all upset," Joe said three hours later, after Gracie had calmed down and resumed her relentless cooking schedule. Seeing how Adam was needed to relieve some of the marshals who'd been on duty while he'd lunched with the family, Joe had volunteered himself as her kitchen helper.

She liked the man. A lot.

In subtle ways, he reminded her of her father whom she so deeply missed. His dry sense of humor. The way for the most part, he just sat back and took things in, making you think he wasn't paying attention to the conversation's ebb and flow until he tossed out a zinger that cracked everyone up. "Gillian means well. Sometimes she just gets a little carried away, trying to solve the world's problems."

"It's okay," Gracie said. "Really. No harm done."

"Good," Joe said, awkwardly slipping his hands in his khaki's pockets. "Anyway, if any taboo subjects should ever again come up—knowing this clan like I do, they no doubt will—please, feel free to tell my wife to mind her own business."

Gracie swallowed fresh tears, doing her best to keep a sharp focus on her bubbling caramel, lightly humming as she stirred.

Actually, now that she'd had time to think about it, this was what family was supposed to be. Loving and concerned. Her parents asked to attend the competition, and at first, she'd agreed, but with Vicente on the loose, the last thing she wanted was to put them in the line of danger.

But then if she felt the competition had the possibility of being dangerous for even spectators, what was she thinking, subjecting not only herself and her baby to the possible line of fire, but also Beau and Adam and this family with whom she'd instantly fallen in love?

"Joe?" she asked, removing the caramel pan from the gas flame.

"Yeah?" he said from the sink where he stood good-naturedly doing her many dishes.

"Do you think I'm being selfish?"

"In regard to what?"

"My insisting upon going through with the competition."

"Not at all. From what little I know of you, you're an amazing cook. The Culinary Olympics were designed to honor and reward chefs with your skill. I think it'd be wrong of you to not go through with it."

"But Caleb clearly seems to think I'm setting up myself and the marshals assigned to me as targets."

"Nah," Joe said, drying a copper-bottomed saucepan. "What you have to know about Caleb is that he's a family guy through and through. He and Allie only recently patched things up after like an eight-year separation. Only then did he meet the son he never knew he had."

"Wow."

"Yeah," Joe said with a sad laugh. "It was a shock to all of us. In a good way. Allie's a judge, and their reunion was a twist of fate, seeing how he was assigned to protect her. She had a couple of close calls—as did his son. I think in steering Beau away from you, he's just trying to protect his brother from his own mistakes."

"Which were?" Gracie asked, smoothing golden caramel onto parchment paper.

"Good question," Joe said with a scratch to his head. "'Cause seeing the three of them as a family now, it looks as if pretty much everything worked out fine. Just like it will for you and your baby." What about Beau? Gracie bit her tongue to keep from asking. Where will he end up in the grand scheme of things? After the trial, would she ever see him again? Or would Caleb's disapproval of their friendship somehow poison him against her?

But then with that last question, was she even being truthful with herself? Whether she wanted to admit it or not, what she and Beau shared went way deeper than mere friendship. She wasn't sure how or when, but somewhere in the past few days, she'd learned to lean on him in so many ways. Not just for the tiny luxuries of when he'd fastened her seat belt or tied her shoes, but like today, when he'd held her through another of what was beginning to feel like far too many crying jags.

"Hey," Joe said softly from behind her. With his hands loosely cupped to her shoulders, he eased her around. "Something you've got to remember is that protecting folks from bad guys is what Caleb, Adam, Beau, and sometimes, Gillian do. In their care, sure, I'm not going to tell you nothing could ever go wrong, but in all probability, the only thing that will mar your competition would be the highly unlikely event of you taking second place."

"HEY, STRANGER," Gracie said, gingerly planting herself alongside Beau on the garden swing. The air was cool and sweet. Chirping crickets sounded a lot perkier than she felt. You know how some women shopped till they dropped? Well, she'd cooked till she'd dropped. It was nine-thirty at night and after having prepped at least twenty, intricate five-course meals since five that morning, her feet and ankles throbbed. "Where've you been all day? I haven't seen you since brunch."

"Here and there," he said, casting her an odd, sideways smile. Not that it wasn't as gorgeous as usual, just that it was strangely vacant. "You always work this hard?"

"Pretty much. Competition among chefs is fierce. Making matters worse is the statistic that somewhere between ninety to ninety-five percent of all restaurants fail within the first year. With that in mind, I can't afford complacency."

"Sure," Beau said, surprised to hear Gracie sounding more like his solely business-minded ex, but with more heart. Bucking those enormous odds took drive he couldn't imagine. The same drive it had taken to lock a marshal in a storage room. Inwardly smiling at that, finding it hard to believe it had happened less than a week earlier, Beau sighed.

"You all right?" she asked, nudging his shoulder. "You seem down."

He shrugged. "I've been worse. Been better. Just one of those days, you know?"

"Want to talk about it? Because if this has anything to do with Caleb wanting me to withdraw from the competition and head back to Portland, the answer's no."

"No one's expecting you to do that. I've explained to Caleb how important this is to your baby's future and he's agreed to back off."

"Then what's his current issue?"

"Truth?" he said with a loaded chuckle. "Me."

Planting an indescribably sweet kiss to his cheek, she said, "What fault could he possibly find with you? I adore you, so obviously, if your brother thinks different, he's the one with problems."

Laughing, Beau slipped his arm around Gracie, tugging her close. He'd never met anyone with whom he could just speak his mind and heart. It was nice. Not feeling like he had to play games. "I like your assessment, although I'm sure Caleb won't."

Linking her fingers with his, she said, "Do I look like I care what your brother thinks? From the start, this mission has been about me and you. First, me trying to outwit you, then, you making me see I need you. My baby needs you."

For the longest time, they just sat there in the milky wash of a perfect crescent moon. Crickets chirped. From far down in the city, came the rumble and clatter of a trolley passing, ringing its bell. But here, now, all that mattered was the two of them, never breaking their stare.

And then Beau leaned forward the slightest bit.

Gracie's breath hitched, then caught. She licked her lips.

He leaned closer still. Closer, closer, until covering

her lips with the sweetest, most exquisitely tender, non-lying kiss she'd ever had. At first his kiss was soft, fragile, tentative until she gave her okay. And when she did by softly sighing his name, he deepened the kiss, gently urging open her mouth, stroking her tongue with his until her breasts ached and tummy tingled and the V between her legs hummed.

"I will protect you," he said.

Dazed, she nodded against him.

He smoothed his fingers down the back of her head.

"It scares me how much you've come to mean in such a short time," she whispered. "I can't even remember what my life was like without you. What does that mean?"

"I don't know," he said, tracing the outline of her lips with his thumb. "I feel the same, but I can't. I tried quitting my job today, so that—"

"You what?" She abruptly sat up. "You're joking, right?"

"No," he said with a sharp laugh. "Hell, no."

"But you only tried quitting? Caleb refused your resignation?"

"Pretty much that's how it went down."

Nodding, she said, "Your brother's a wise man. I'd be furious if I ever found out you'd quit a great job you're obviously good at for me."

"Yeah, but don't you get it? I couldn't see any other way for us to find out if what we're feeling is real."

"What do you think?" She was almost afraid to ask.

Lips pressed tight, he said, "I don't know. I thought I did, but then Caleb showed up and Gillian and even Allie threw in her two cents on the matter. The general consensus is that everyone adores you, but thinks I'm moving too fast. That somehow, because of what happened with my ex, I'm confusing things. Mixing you up with her and finding emotion where ordinarily there would be none."

"O-okay…" Gracie said, subtlety inching away. "Mind telling me what happened with your ex? You know, just so I'll be up to speed."

Beau did tell her—details about the breakup he'd never told another soul. About how Ingrid told him she'd only agreed to marry him to make her older, savvier partner jealous. "Can you believe it, she wanted to deliver a wake-up call to the guy that she wouldn't stay on the market long. Up till our wedding day, she'd expected Kevin to come running to the rescue, but when he didn't, she'd figured what the hell? Why not give me a shot? At least I was good in bed."

"She actually said that?" Gracie asked, leaning forward in rapt interest, experiencing Beau's still raw pain as her own. "What a bitch."

"Wait—it gets worse." He told her about the baby. How for seven months, he'd been on top of the world, thinking he was on the verge of finally becoming a father only to fall when the truth became known.

"I'm so sorry," Gracie said, tossing her arms around Beau, hugging for all she was worth. "But as awful as going through all of that had to be, I still don't get the connection between me and your ex. What? Do we look alike?"

"No way," Beau said. "The bulging belly's as far as any resemblance goes. But my family thinks just because you're pregnant, I've formed an attachment to you I wouldn't ordinarily have if we'd just met at a coffee house or bar."

"I suppose it would make sense," she said, eyes wet and shimmering, "but in here—" she patted her chest "—I think I would've sensed you weren't sincere. And it's funny, but I have doubts, too. You know, about how we hardly know each other, and how I'm barely out of a disastrous relationship. The last thing on my mind should be kissing another man. But Beau..." She cradled his dear face in her hands. "God help me, but aside from cooking, kissing you is the only thing I can think about."

"God *help* you?" Snatching her hands, kissing her palms, grinning, he said, "You say that as if wanting to kiss me is a bad thing."

"According to Caleb, it is, isn't it?"

"Hmm..." A teasing smile played along the corners of his lips.

"I'll need another sample to be fully qualified to judge for myself."

"Sounds fun," he said with a sexy growl, nuzzling the base of her throat. "You smell good. Like garlic and Worcestershire and all that normalcy you keep talking about."

"How long do you think till we find it, Beau? Normalcy?"

"We?" He looked up, fixing her with his intense brown stare. "As in, the two of us?"

She brushed his cheek with her thumb, suddenly feeling proprietary, needful of marking her territory, even if the marking was only to reassure herself. "I don't know," she said with a shrug. "After all of this is over, I think the two of us are at least worth additional exploration."

"Exploration, huh?" He went back to nuzzling. "I've always enjoyed a challenging expedition."

"Oh, now I'm an expedition? A challenging one at that?"

"Let's see," he said, roving his kisses up her neck and jaw and chin and cheeks. "Since knowing you, I've been shot, nearly put in the slammer and/or fired. That sound challenging to you?"

"Nah." Casting him her biggest grin, she shook her head. "If I were truly a challenge, I'd've made you devein shrimp for eight hours or mince a bushel of onions or maybe paint my toenails."

"Oh, sure," he said, returning her grin along with a big nod. "How could I have forgotten those unthankful tasks?"

Though he was smiling, the gesture didn't carry through to his eyes. Not even close. What still haunted him? His ex? His argument with his brother? If what she felt for Beau was truly the start of something serious, maybe the responsible thing would be letting him go. Let him do his job, while she focused solely on hers. They could sort their issues after the trial. But while that sounded good in theory, in reality, she wasn't sure she could make it through the competition and trial without him.

"Ready for bed?" he asked, toying with a curl.

Not wanting to press him, hoping he'd open up to her in time, in his own way, she swallowed hard and nodded.

He kissed her on her forehead, then rose from the swing, holding out his hands to help her.

He smiled. And it was a big, warm, wonderful smile full of his strong white teeth and the promise that he above all other men she'd known was different. Better. In every conceivable way. He would never lie to her. Or betray her. He would just be.

Solid as that proverbial rock.

Predictable as the rising sun.

Yet even as she knew all that, goose bumps rose on her forearms. Something about Beau had changed in the short time they'd been outside.

But what?

He looked the same. Essentially acted the same. But he wasn't. A light had gone off inside him.

Now, the only question was why?

Chapter Eleven

"Caleb? Can I talk to you for a sec?"

Later that night, Beau stood in the library's shadows, watching his brother work on a report.

"Sure," Caleb said, putting down his pen to rub his temples with his thumb and forefingers. "What's on your mind."

"First off, I want to apologize. I said some out-of-line things, and I'm sorry."

"Thanks. Me, too," Caleb said, easing back in a burgundy leather swivel chair. "We good?"

"Yeah." Beau helped himself to the guest chair alongside the massive mahogany desk. "But there is one more thing." He slapped his star on the desk. The room was so quiet save for the incessant tick of a grandfather clock, that the sound of metal hitting wood struck Beau as thunderous.

Caleb raised his eyebrows.

"I don't want this to be permanent," Beau said. "In

fact, as soon as this cooking gig is over, and we head back to Portland, if it's all right with Franks, I'd like to be assigned to another case. One in which I'm able to be more objective."

Caleb shoved the star back across the desk. "Keep it," he said. "I'll handle things with Franks. Consider yourself on vacation until we get back to Portland next week Monday."

"Thanks," Beau said, releasing air he hadn't even realized he'd been holding.

"Thank you," Caleb said. "You're doing the right thing—for both of you."

"Yeah." Beau nodded, then pushed to his feet. The sooner he ended this meeting with Caleb, the sooner he could plan how to woo Gracie without leaving the house. He was almost out of the library when he turned. "Oh—and Caleb?"

"Yeah?"

"Can we keep this matter private from Gracie? I think she'd feel she was somehow to blame, when in actuality, it's all me." Gracie said she'd be furious if she ever heard he'd quit—even temporarily—for her. But if he played his cards right, hopefully, she'd never find out. "You said some profound things this afternoon—not especially kind, but stuff that got me thinking. Even if Gracie wasn't in the picture, I'm probably long overdue for some time to get my head back in a good place."

"I'm proud of you," Caleb said. "And I know

Dad will be, too. Who knows, maybe Gracie is the woman for you? Stranger things have happened. And one thing's for sure, with her around, we'll all start eating better."

After sharing a laugh, Beau again thanked his older, wiser brother, then started his first vacation in years.

"YECH," Beau said in regard to Gracie's Algerian egg and meatball soup.

Granted, at seven in the morning, it might be a tad early for such a dish, but surely it wasn't that bad? Gracie eyed him for a moment before taking a bite herself, then gagging. "Tastes like dead night crawlers."

"How do you know how a dead night crawler tastes?" he asked, taking the pot from the stove to dump the contents down the disposal. Adam had been assigned door duty, leaving Beau as her official kitchen helper. So far, though, he'd been more trouble than help. Not that he wasn't doing a great job of helping her chop, dice, slice and keep up with dishwashing, just that his nearness set off all manner of needs. Needs for more kissing and touching and generally getting to know him in *every* way a man and woman can.

"My dad used to take me fishing," she said. "He had this old truck with an even older camper shell attached to the bed. Mom refused to step foot in it. She didn't want me to, either—said it was contaminated. With what, she never said. But the smell—it was a lot like that soup tasted." A ghostly smile playing about her lips, she patted her stomach. "I'm excited about my baby meeting him. Dad. He's a good man. Rotten fisherman, but a great dad. You'll like him."

"He know what you're going through? About the trial?" he asked while she helped herself to a bite of delicious Croatian spinach pie.

"Sure. And he and Mom are planning to be out here for that. But as for the specifics of Vicente hiring guys to shoot at us and then kidnapping me—no," she said with a fork to her mouth. "He and Mom would freak. I figure it's one of those things best left to sharing the highlights with them once it's over."

"Think that's fair? Don't they have a right to know? To help out?"

"What're they going to do?" No longer hungry, she shoved her plate aside, ready to lose herself in preparing yet another dish. "Apply for gun permits and take down Vicente themselves? Why would they do that when I have you and the rest of your gang?"

He didn't answer. Didn't even look at her.

"Let's get started on the next recipe," she said, suddenly on edge. "I'm ready to get Algeria over with."

Her back to Beau, Gracie shuffled through her cards to find her recipe for *Kesksou Bil Djedj* or in English, Algerian couscous.

"Hey," Beau said, stepping up behind her, easing his arms around her waist, resting his hands on her belly. "Did I do or say something to tick you off?"

Eyes closed, she leaned against him, loving the feel of him cocooning her in his strength. "It's nothing you said. It's just that every time I remember you and I aren't just hanging out together in a fabulous apartment because we want to be, but because we have to, it makes me furious all over again. I want Vicente locked away for the rest of his miserable life."

"Me, too, sweetie." Beau kissed the top of her head. "Me, too."

Gracie started gathering the items needed for her next recipe, but her heart wasn't in it. Truthfully she was exhausted. With the baby and all—not to mention the emotional and physical toll competition preparation was taking—she tried putting up an energetic front, but after each action-filled day it was getting harder. "You want to take a break?"

"Depends. Can you afford the time off?"

Popping the chicken breasts she'd been about to skin, bone and cube into the fridge, she said, "I'm thinking this is one of those things I can't afford *not* to do. Come on," she said, forcing a bright smile. "Let's hit the pool."

"You sure?"

No. Suddenly she wasn't sure of anything. Least of all her curious relationship with Marshal Beau. But then nothing else in her life currently made sense, why should her growing affection for him?

"Yeah," she said. "I'm sure…" Sure she wanted

to have fun again and remember what it felt like to be free. Normal. "Sure, last one in has to kiss the other's feet!"

LAUGHING Gracie beat Beau to the water, but she was pretty sure the only reason for this was that the stairwell leading up to the rooftop garden and pool was so narrow he couldn't get around her.

"I win!" she said, sticking out her tongue at Beau and the sweltering day by tossing her robe onto a deck chair, then taking a running jump into the sparkling pool.

Beau barreled in, too.

"That was a dirty trick," he said, swimming up beside her. "You deliberately blocked that hall."

"Like I could've magically shrunk my belly?" Had she known how hot Marshal Beau looked wearing nothing but the cargo shorts he was using as swim trunks, she might've thought twice about accompanying him to the pool.

The man's chest was rock-hard and tan and glistening in the sun. She wanted to run her hands all over that chest, committing every sinewy ridge to memory. In raising her gaze to his face, she'd thought she'd be in a far safer zone, but water droplets clung to the slight stubble shadowing his jaw, glistening there and in the short spikes of his dark hair.

His gunshot wound was healing nicely now that he regularly took his antibiotic, but seeing the greenish bruise reminded her whose fault it was that he'd been hurt.

Hers.

But she didn't want to think about that now. Not with everything else about the day being perfect.

The air smelled of chlorine and the coconut tanning oil Allie loaned her. The only thing that would make the setting better was the enticing smell of burgers sizzling on the poolside grill. Or maybe if the rest of Beau's family had joined them. Not that she didn't love being alone with Beau— aside from the marshals lurking just beyond the thick hedge ensuring the pool's privacy, but in hanging out with Beau's family, she'd have felt acceptance from them. As it was, though they'd all been incredibly kind and polite, she wasn't sure what they made of her and Beau's sudden feelings for each other.

The sheer normalcy of the enchanting setting might've reduced Gracie to tears if she hadn't been so darned determined to continue with the plan she'd set in motion just a short while earlier. The plan to steal at least a part of the day for herself.

This was no time for tears, but laughter and fun.

With the cool water cocooning her like liquid silk, supporting her awkward size and weight, she felt like a kid again. Like a hopeful, ever-dreaming teenager giddy over her upcoming Saturday night date.

Eyes closed, treading water, she tilted her head to the sun, loving the hot/cold contrast of the drops evaporating on her face.

She raised up to find Beau staring, grinning in that naughty way she'd so grown to love.

"What're you thinking?" she dared ask.

"How pretty you are." But how could he be thinking that, when she'd thought the same about him? "And how much I'd like to kiss not only those cute little feet of yours, but your lips."

"Think your boss would approve?"

He shrugged.

"I say go for it." Suddenly, selfishly, she swam one, smooth stroke his way.

"Oh, you would, would you?"

Grinning, she nodded.

"And if I for once decide to behave? Keep my hands—and lips—to myself?"

"Then I'd just—" she pressed her lips to his, instantly aroused by the feel of their wet, slick legs and toes touching beneath the water's undulating surface "—kiss you."

Fortunately for her, Beau was standing, leaving her free to wrap her arms around his neck, drowning in the serious waves of pleasure he was causing with his tongue.

He drew back. "Guess not knowing which of my brothers or coworkers are watching, we should keep this G-rated."

"Yeah," she said, struggling to speak past serious need. "S'pose we should."

Still, so she wasn't entirely adrift, as required by the terms of their bet, he did kiss both her feet. "What do you want to do instead?"

"You mean instead of kissing?" Nothing. At the moment, there was nothing in the whole, wide world she'd rather do than kiss him and hold him and—

"Come on," he said, releasing her to slice through sparkling water to the pool's blue tile rim. He pushed himself out. Forever imprinting her brain with the image of his muscled shoulders and back and—*oh my.* The sight of those wet cargo shorts hugging his buns nearly left her crying for a lifeguard!

"Well?" He turned to face her, hands on his hips. "Aren't you coming?"

"To do what?" she asked. "I'm comfy here." Where all he could see of her was her head, which had apparently passed muster. Trouble was, in her current very pregnant state, the rest of her blossoming body left a lot to be desired. She surely couldn't compete with some of the bathing beauties a guy as hunky as he must've dated over the years.

"You'll be just as *comfy* where we're going."

Rolling her eyes, she sighed, then paddled to the nearest ladder, hoisting herself out, hating the sensation of gravity returning. As weightless as she'd been in the pool, she now felt humongous.

Bloated and big and tired and—

"Took you long enough," Beau said, reaching for her hand.

"Don't," she said, brushing him away. "I have to get my robe."

"Why? It's hot as hell out here."

"Just because." She crossed her arms over breasts that seemed twice their normal size. What had possessed her to ever even buy this maternity swimsuit? Granted, she'd thought it might be relaxing to swim in between competition rounds, but now, she could see she'd been completely, totally—

"Come on." He took her hand, lacing their fingers, stroking her palm with the tip of his thumb. Muddying her mind with his mere touch. "I promise even without your robe, you'll like this."

She trailed after him, and since she was already in the realm of make-believe in this glorious garden setting, why not go further? And pretend that look he'd given her after they'd kissed, the one that for a minute anyway, had made her think he'd actually wanted more, was how he really felt. Like he'd anticipated them taking kissing to the next level, behind closed doors.

Her hand still in his, he led her down a sun-dappled, winding stone path lined with fragrant honeysuckle and snapdragons.

"This is beautiful," she said about the unexplored portion of the roof. "How'd you find it?"

"I didn't. Adam did."

"Remind me to thank him," she said with an easy grin. "So what's at the end?"

He led them from the shady trail into an open space on the roof's far corner. "Surprise!"

"Oh, Beau…"

Beau had to chuckle at the sight of Gracie staring at the one-of-a-kind garden where flowers had been planted to represent different foods, and shrubs carved into fun food shapes like hamburgers and three-tiered wedding cakes and a drumstick.

At the garden's center was a massive pepperoni pizza made of what had to be thousands of mozzarella cheese-colored flowers dotted with round clumps of pepperoni-red blossoms. Perfectly browned pebbles made the crust.

"You don't close that mouth of yours," Beau teased, "a bee's going to fly in."

That earned him a halfhearted swat. "Hush," she said. "You're spoiling it. Look." She released his hand to run off to another of the gardener's creations. "Look at that fruit bowl… How much time went into just the lemons? I can't imagine how long it must've taken for the grapes. I'll bet the gardener who made this doesn't wile away his afternoons lazing around a pool. I should be studying. You're a bad influence, Marshal Beau."

"True, but wasn't taking a break your idea?"

She blushed. "You didn't have to agree with me, though. Meaning you *are* a bad influence."

"Thanks," he said with a slow grin.

"Only you would take what was meant as an insult and turn it into a compliment."

"Seriously…" Facing her, hands on her shoulders, he said, "What happens if you don't win?"

"Poverty. Debilitating depression. The usual."

"No, really," he said. "Got a backup plan?"

Tucking those roving hands of his into his pockets, he said, "Not that it's any of my business, but it seems like you're pinning an awful lot on this single contest. Seems like it might be more practical to get a loan."

"Oh, even with the prize money, I'll still have to do that. Winning would be a nice financial cushion. In the event I don't win, don't think for a second I'll give up. I'll just work for someone else for a while before starting up another place of my own."

Wandering hand in hand with her down the elaborate rows, Beau asked, "So you prefer being your own boss?"

"Doesn't everyone?" she asked with a wink.

They strolled in companionable silence while around them, day breathed a long sigh into the approaching night. Hot air turned sultry. Cicadas picked up where song birds had let off.

"Know what I'd like?" Gracie said while they wound their way back to the pool.

"Name it and it's yours."

"I was just wanting to take another swim, but since you're in a generous mood…" She grinned.

"I'll take a new restaurant and a sweet little house for me and the baby, and—"

"What about me? Do I get my own room, or just share with you?"

"Beau…What are you doing? You know as well as I do that after Vicente's trial, it's over for us. You'll be assigned to some new damsel in distress. I'll find something to do, but—"

"Stop," he said, pausing to face her, easing his hands around her waist. One look into his sinfully gorgeous dark eyes and her pulse raced faster than the last time she'd nearly been shot. "What's happening between us—the chemistry—has nothing to do with my job. I've been a deputy marshal for going on ten years, and in that time, I've protected a lot of nice folks. Many of them women. Never once, in all those assignments, have I ever felt half what I feel right now for you."

"Why?"

"Huh?"

"Is that such a tough thing to answer?"

He released her to toss up his hands. "What do you think? I mean, that's like me asking you why you like to cook."

"That's easy. Because I enjoy pleasing people. Seeing the looks on their faces when something I've made for but one second makes them forget everything but the simple pleasure of sitting down for a meal."

"Okay then…" Hands on her shoulders, he said, "I like you because of your crazy-curl hair and gorgeous blue eyes and your smile that lights up a room. Because of the bravery you've shown in following through with a dream no matter how much your ex tried to stop you. I like you because of your endearing habit of humming under your breath while you stir, and because your brownies are far better than my last round of sex. And—"

Laughing, she said, "Okay, okay, that's enough. You're embarrassing me."

"Why does knowing how fantastic you are embarrass you?" he asked, taking her hands to kiss the pounding pulse points on her wrists.

"Because after the disastrous marriage I've quite literally had to struggle to survive. In finding you in such a serendipitous way, I feel overly blessed. And like none of what we're feeling is real. Like if I blink you'll vanish, and Vicente will be back, holding a gun to my head."

They'd reached the pool, and the water was glassy and serene. The air smelled faintly of chlorine and sunbaked concrete.

Tears glistened in her eyes, filing him with urges like wanting to protect her not just for the duration of Vicente's trial, but forever.

"You're safe," he said softly, pulling her into his arms. "No more thinking of the past. Only on what a great future you and your baby are going to have." Kneeling before her, he pressed a dozen kisses to her belly.

"I—I know," she said. "I know I've got to put him out of my mind. Dwelling on what might happen isn't healthy for me or the baby, but Beau…" Staring at him, helplessly fluttering her hands at her sides, she shook her head. "I don't know what else to do. If I for one second give in to the reality of my life, I—" She laughed through tears. "I don't know what I'll do. Have some kind of attack or just…flip out."

"No," he said, rising to draw her into another hug. "You're too strong for that."

"You think?" She snorted. "That just goes to show how little you truly know about me. I'm a mess inside. Where most people have courage, I have chocolate pudding."

"Mmm…" he said, nipping at the sensitive spot just beneath her left ear. "I've always had a fondness for that stuff."

"I'm serious," she complained, all the same, leaning into his nuzzle, scrunching her neck.

"Me, too…"

"We ever going swimming?"

She was changing the subject, and for once, Beau was glad. It was shaping up to be a beautiful night, and he didn't want to waste a minute more of it focusing on her scumbag ex.

"Yeah," he said. "Let's go swimming." And while they were at it, pray they never again encountered human sharks.

"BUT WE HAVE TO have been in here going on a couple hours," Beau complained.

Gracie ignored him, happily paddling along on her back, loving the song of the crickets. "If you had any idea how heavy I feel outside this pool, and how light I feel in it, you'd understand."

He swam up behind her, scooping her into his arms. "Guess what I am?"

"A meanie for wanting me to get out?"

He made an obnoxious buzzer sound. "I'm the pool vac, coming to suck up all the flotsam and debris." He made slurpy/sucking noises at the base of her throat.

"That's mean!" she cried. "I'm not debris!"

He inspected her shriveled fingers. "At the very least, as badly as you've pruned, you're an entire new species of fruit."

She stuck out her tongue. "Shows what you know. Fruit doesn't have species, but varieties."

"With all your wriggling and jiggling, you'd for sure be a species. A hot one." He winked.

She swatted.

Hand cupping her cheek, he brushed water from her eyebrows with the pad of his thumb. "For debris, you're very sexy."

"No," she said with a firm shake of her head. "I'm lots of things, but not that."

"Don't," he said, kissing her closed eyes, the tip

of her nose. "Please don't ever talk that way about yourself."

"I used to not," she said. "I used to feel sexy, glamorous, desired. But then…"

"I know. And we don't have to go there. Not ever."

"Thank you for that."

"God, I'd like to kiss you."

"Why don't you?" she said, her breath coming at a funny, hitching pace.

"Do you even have to ask? If I start kissing you, I'm afraid I won't be able to stop."

She leaned up to kiss him. "Who said I want you to—stop, I mean."

"But what you went through. You've gotta be fragile."

"In here," she said, patting her heart. "Yeah. Very fragile. But that's where you come in. You've gradually been making me strong."

Beau groaned. How had she known those were exactly the words he'd needed to hear? That the drastic decision he'd made in even temporarily leaving his job to explore his feelings for a woman he barely knew, yet felt like he'd forever known, hadn't been dumb.

"Well?" she asked. "I thought I was getting kissed?" She raised that bossy little chin of hers, challenging him with a sin-sexy pout.

"Woman," he said with a growl. "Tonight, you're not just getting kissed, but reborn."

ROUND ABOUT MIDNIGHT, long after sharing pizza and two agonizingly long movies with Beau's family, Gracie closed her eyes as he eased beside her onto her room's jumbo, circular bed.

"Took you long enough," she teased.

"Tell me about it. I had to wait for my nosy sister and brother-in-law to go to bed. Allie's still up reading court briefs, but at least Caleb's zonked. Your on-duty marshals are all strategically posted—hopefully for the rest of the night."

"You officially off duty?"

"Uh-huh," he said, slipping his hand into her robe, skimming his warm, rough palm along her collarbone to her shoulder, easing a few fingers under the thin chemise she wore as a bra.

She froze.

"You okay?" he asked.

Nodding, she said, "Sure."

"Then why are you all of the sudden so tense?"

"Maybe we should turn out the chandelier? It's too bright."

"'Kay." He pushed himself up, switching off the gaudy crystal chandelier's dimmer. The room's only light now spilled in a long, yellow rectangle through the partially closed bathroom door. "Better?"

She nodded, only it wasn't, so she squeezed her eyes shut tighter.

"Baby, if it's any darker, I'll need one of those little miner lights mounted on my forehead to find all your equipment."

"Sorry. I just—" She rolled onto her side. "When Vicente…Th-that last time he…He just barged into my apartment. It was broad daylight, and I kept thinking how could this be happening? It isn't really happening." Tears streamed down her cheeks and she hugged herself for comfort, but then Beau was there, pulling her against him, blocking the light, the awful memories.

"After all that swimming," he eventually said, "you've got to be beat. Let me get that bathroom light and we'll call it a night."

"But—"

He pressed the softest, most gentle kiss to her lips any woman could ever hope for. A kiss so surreal in its perfection that if she hadn't been able to reach out and test Beau's solidity, she'd have feared him and his kiss a dream.

"When you're ready," he said, "you'll know. Until then, let's sleep."

"But after all that making out in the pool, you probably think I'm a tease. Or that—"

"The only thing I think is that your ex is a monster."

Clutching the sheets to her neck, Gracie sighed.

On that point, she and Beau very much agreed.

No wonder she so badly craved the gift of being normal. Because after the nightmare Vicente had put her through, she was only just beginning to see how abnormal she'd truly become.

Chapter Twelve

Gracie woke sometime in the middle of the night to find Beau only partially covered in the sheet and thin blanket, wholly covered in a perfect wash of moonlight.

Just glancing at him, at his dear, handsome features and toned body that had alternately protected her and brought her such pleasure, left her knowing that if she were to ever become whole again, she'd have to take the first step.

It wasn't someone else's responsibility to fix her, but her own.

Not that what had happened with Vicente had in any way been her fault, but like Beau had said earlier, this was her night to be reborn. She was a grown woman with a woman's needs. Before Vicente took her that last time against her will, before their divorce, they'd enjoyed a healthy sex life. He wasn't the only man she'd ever been with, but now, gazing upon a man she'd somehow, almost accidentally, grown to love, she knew Beau would most likely be the last man she'd ever make love with.

For if she lived through Vicente's trial, only to have to then say goodbye to Beau, she wasn't sure if her heart could withstand the pain.

Seeing him sprawled across the bed like this, wearing nothing but dark boxers, he was her every fantasy come to life.

Launching a brave exploratory mission, she ran her hand along six-pack abs. Along his equally well-defined chest. He was beautiful. Sheer perfection both inside and out.

On her knees, bracing her hands on either side of him, she kissed him, right over his slowly beating heart. If he knew she was awake, watching him, wanting him, would his pulse race like hers?

She planted more kisses up the length and width of his chest, skimmed her hand lower. Over muscular thighs and back to the swelling bulge between those thighs.

Just the head of him pushed through the slat in his boxers. It was healthy and pink and not the least bit threatening, and so she held it, caressed it. Fondled and kissed it until he groaned, writhing in the bed.

"Grace?" He raised slightly only to drop back down, groaning again. "What're you doing? It's got to be like two or three in the morn—oh…Whoa." He slid his fingers into the hair at the back of her head, encouraging her to follow through with her current course—wherever that may lead. "You sure about this?"

"Uh-huh," she said in a voice so raspy with passion, she barely recognized it as her own.

"But, Grace, earlier you—"

"Shh…" Straddling him, she put her fingers to his lips. "I don't want to talk anymore, just feel." He was rock-hard and throbbing against her. But that wasn't enough. Not nearly enough. She wanted him pulsing inside her.

"Ah, sure. I've probably got a condom in my wallet. Want me to get it?"

She shook her head, already reaching for the bedside table.

"It's in—"

"Bingo," she said, holding up her prize.

"Want me to—"

Before he could even ask if she wanted him to put it on, she had it out of the wrapper and rolled down his length.

"Gracie, shouldn't we—"

Blocking his objection, she climbed off him to loosen the belt on the silky robe she'd put on after their last lovemaking attempt, then slipped off her panties before climbing back on top of his erection, swallowing him whole.

Eyes closed, shutting out the moonlight, the faint chirp of crickets, she focused on nothing but Beau, on the feeling of fullness and joy and completion he brought to her life.

Her robe fell open and he planted his hands on her hips, helping her down, bringing them closer, ever closer.

A part of her told her to hide, to belt up her robe and shut herself in the bathroom for the rest of the night. But the part of her tired of hiding from the truth, from the fact that no matter what Vicente had done, she was still a woman, desirable and beautiful and strong, rode on. That part—the strong part—allowed her robe to whisper from her shoulders, pooling on the backs of her calves. That part willed her hands to Beau's, guiding them up to her full, aching breasts.

The harder she rode, the greater the pleasure, the certainty that nowhere on earth or in time had she ever been more secure. Taking Beau's hand to her mouth, nipping, licking, sucking his fingers, she drove out the demons and let in the light. So much glorious, beautiful light.

Chills rose on her forearms.

Her nipples puckered and hardened.

An orgasm hit hard and white-hot, leaving her quivering with emotion.

His came a few seconds after.

"I—I love you," she cried. "Thank you, thank you. I was so afraid of never feeling anything again. But then you came along…"

"I should be thanking you," he said, smoothing

curls back from her cheeks. He cast an ultrasexy grin her way, fluttering her stomach. "I love you, too."

Grinning right back at him, she said, "I've never done anything like that before. I already feel such a deep connection between us, but I guess I'm greedy and wanted more."

"You're not greedy," he said, smoothing his hands along her belly. "Just understandably overwhelmed by my manliness."

Laughing, swatting him, Gracie awkwardly made her way off the bed, then held out her hand. "Care to join me in a bubble bath?"

Rising, curving his fingers around hers, he said, "Heck, yeah."

SITTING WAIST-DEEP in the oversize tub, Gracie softly snoring with her cheek resting on his chest, Beau couldn't remember having ever felt more at peace. So much so, that he'd said the "L" word back there without it even being a conscious thought—just that he did love Gracie. Yes, it was way too fast. Crazy. Unrealistic. But from where he was sitting, it was also undeniable.

Toying with a curl, he wondered if he'd be getting ahead of himself by going out sometime later than three in the morning to buy an engagement ring. Probably. But the way he felt consumed by emotion for this precious woman, he couldn't wait to officially make her—and her baby—his own.

What you feel for Gracie isn't real. It's hyped-up emotions brought on by danger and all that love you still have for a son or daughter who just wasn't meant to be.

Brows furrowed, Beau refused to let Caleb's negativity rain on his and Gracie's parade.

What they'd just shared had been beautiful. Way beyond the realm of casual sex and into a spiritual place he'd never before been. He knew like he knew his own name that what he felt for Gracie wasn't leftover wishes for what might've been with Ingrid, but the real deal.

Plain and simple, they were in love. And just as soon as Gracie's life settled down, Beau damn well planned to make her his wife.

No one was going to stand in the way of that. Not Caleb, not Vicente and certainly not the ghosts of either of their disastrous pasts.

FOR GRACIE, the next two days passed in a content, but hectic, blur. Apart from the cooking, there were the contest preparations, consisting of making plenty of lists and checking them twice, and sending Allie and Gillian on missions deep into the heart of Chinatown and beyond to purchase many of the exotic spices she was allowed as part of her supplies. Everything including whole juniper berries for the spicy, pinelike touch they added to rich game and asafoetida, which the shopping duo had been warned to keep in an airtight container to protect everything else from its rotting onion smell. The spice wasn't something she enjoyed using, but would be crucial should she draw an area of India populated by Brahmin and Jain castes.

Beside her through it all, calming her, encouraging her, was Beau. Whenever she felt too tired to carry on, he was there, even going so far as to try new dishes for her by following her directions while she lounged on a chaise he'd hauled into the center of the kitchen from her room—or would that be their room, seeing how he secretly shared it with her each night.

And now, as she entered the competition's bustling registration and press area, held in the sumptuous Hotel Dominican's burgundy ballroom, she squeezed Beau's hand so tightly she was surprised he didn't complain about being hurt.

Though his fellow marshals had discreetly surrounded her—including Gillian who looked so different with her somber game face on—Gracie felt nervous, yet strangely serene. Like she'd been working up for this her whole life, and here it was. Her destiny about to unfold—with the event made even more exciting by the man by her side. Having her parents with her, too, would have been the cherry on top, but—

"Gracie? Honey? Is that you?"

Mom?

Gracie looked to her left to find her parents strolling toward her, both looking slightly older, but essentially as she'd remembered. Her father tall, graying with a small bulge at his waist, and her mother, petite and stylish in black slacks and a pale pink T-shirt emblazoned with *Go Chef Gracie*.

Instantly teary upon being reunited with her family, she gave Beau a hug, too, once her mother relayed that it had been him who'd made the travel arrangements.

Hugs and introductions were shared—those with the on-duty members of the Logue clan brief, and then the whole lot of them accompanied her on a dizzying round of interviews. Questions ranged from what country was she most hoping to first draw to what was her own favorite dish. Several more brazen reporters inquired as to the status of Vicente. Had she been in contact with him since his prison break? To them, she politely, but firmly said no comment, allowing Beau to steer her away.

FROM A RELATIVELY quiet corner of the Hotel Dominican's Grand Ballroom, a disguised Vicente smiled. So nice that before she died, his wife would share one last reunion with her family.

Vicente, a direct descendant of Bolivian royalty, had never cared for his in-laws. Their love of flea markets, home remodeling and beer struck him as base. He saw it as a miracle that someone as genteel as Gracie had been born of their loins. At least at one time Gracie had been genteel. But then she'd betrayed him. What had she been thinking, turning over his private diaries to police? The pain she'd brought him by her lack of support had been crushing.

But soon—very soon—it would be her turn to hurt.

FRIDAY MORNING, Gracie had a devil of a time concentrating on her El Salvadorian *Pupusas Revueltas* when her every nerve ending felt electrified from just Beau's presence. Glancing over her shoulder, she grinned, thrilled judges had okayed her last minute petition to add him to her team. Contestants were allowed one assistant, and while she hadn't at first planned on using anyone—not because she hadn't wanted help, but because there had been no one to ask. After the last few days spent working together in the safe house kitchen, she and Beau had begun to feel like a well-oiled team.

Softly humming, she stirred her flour and water mixture faster, glad this was to be her next to last dish of the flurried round. While drawing El Salvador hadn't been her first choice, it wasn't too terribly hard, and she was familiar enough with the regional specialties to showcase a nice array of dishes, including two main dishes, *Ceviche de Camarones,* which was essentially lime-cooked shrimp, and *Carne Asada*, which was grilled steak. Accompanying those, were *Chiles Rellenos*, *Frijoles Refritos, Curtido Salvadoreno* and *Plátanos Fritos*. The *pupusas* she was currently working on made for a nice bread. And for dessert, she'd prepared a simple, yet sumptuous flan.

"Do you have any idea how sexy you look when you stir?"

"Hush," she said, shooting him an over-her-shoulder grin.

He hovered behind her, not so close that to the casual observer they would look unprofessional, but definitely close enough that her every nerve ending was aware of his heat and masculine scent and sheer size that made her feel small, yet protected.

"Thirty-minute warning!" The first round judge called.

Mixing and mixing, Gracie found herself hurrying to finish not because she was tired, but because she couldn't wait to corral Beau in the private storage area behind her kitchen to sample a few of his specialties—like neck kissing and ear kissing and her favorite, French kissing!

The day had been a dream. No sign of Vicente or his men. Nothing but anticipation for hoping the judges enjoyed her offerings enough to send her to the next preliminary round.

"Here," Beau said, taking Gracie's bowl. "Let me do that."

"Thanks." Gracie moved on to the *Curtido Salvadoreno*, trying to focus on the task at hand. But when she lifted the lid on blanched cabbage, hot, moist air kissed her hand, returning her to that night in the pool when Beau had kissed a trail from her palm to her lips. When they'd made love, she'd missed that—not being able to kiss him, but the size of her belly had kind of made it hard to—

"What next, boss?"

Reddening, Gracie looked up. "Um, how about rolling the flour mixture into balls."

"Yes, ma'am."

"Beau?" she asked from the stove.

"Yeah?"

"In case I forget to tell you later, thank you—for everything. Not just helping me here at the competition, but for getting me in a secure mental place. I'm so happy, I—" With the back her hand, she swiped at a few goofy sentimental tears. "I'm just so happy I could burst."

He winked. "If you have to burst, please wait until after the round. I've worked too damned hard on all of this stuff to have you ruining our chances at this late hour."

She stuck out her tongue.

"Honey," Gracie's mom said, holding her hand as they stood in the bustling ballroom, awaiting the judges' announcement on which half of the 193 contestants would move to the next round. The cacophony of raised voices all talking at once would've been exhausting had Gracie not been so hyped up herself, eagerly awaiting results. Chaotic,

New Age jazz playing over loudspeakers didn't do much for creating an overall calming atmosphere, either. "I'm so excited for you. I just know you're going to win."

Gracie gave her mom a brief hug. "I've got a good feeling, too, but I think being too confident would jinx me."

"You just let your father and me and Beau be confident for you."

"What do you think of him?" Gracie asked, eyeing Beau and her dad as they stood in a mile-long cash bar line. White wine for her folks, and she was having sparkling water. Same for Beau, seeing how he was on duty. Thank God. She'd have been so upset had he quit his job for her.

"I've got to say, on first impressions, he seems like an amazing man. But do you think you're moving a little fast? You know, considering the baby and all you've been through with Vicente?"

"Probably," she said, worrying her lower lip. "The whole thing has been sort of surreal. Our meeting was strange from the start, but, Mom, I can't help myself. I feel drawn to him. Like he may be the one."

Her mother frowned.

"What?" Gracie asked.

Hand on Gracie's forearm, her mother softened her voice. "Honey, not so long ago, you said the same thing about Vicente. Be careful, that's all."

While Gracie knew her mother meant well, she

wished she'd butt out. Yes, she and Beau hardly knew each other. It seemed everyone around them delighted in pointing out this fact. But another fact—one all these seemingly well-meaning folks failed to notice was that she and Beau were inexplicably in love. And happy. What was so wrong with that? Both of them had already been through so much. Didn't they deserve happiness in their lives?

Yes! her heart cried.

But the realist in Gracie, the part of her who had been to hell and back with Vicente, sickeningly wondered if her mother could be right.

"Here you go," Beau said, handing Gracie her water, and her mother, wine.

"Mmm…" her mother said, sipping with both hands on her glass. "Thank you, Beau."

"You're welcome."

"How is it," she asked him, "that you're on duty, but are allowed to socialize?"

"Seniority perk," he said with a wink.

"Sign me up," Gracie's father said. "Getting paid for hanging out with these two beauties sounds like a good deal to me." Snagging Gracie's mom about her waist, he pulled her in for a kiss. As a teenager, it used to gross Gracie out, seeing her parents being affectionate. But now it made her glad, hopeful that she might one day be as content.

On the competition award podium, a tall, slender blonde dressed all in black, tapped the microphone and the jazz was abruptly turned off. "Attention, please! May I please have your attention?"

The once boisterous crowd fell quiet.

"My name is Freddy Turner, and I'm the chair of this year's Culinary Arts Invitational…" She paused for a polite round of applause, then said, "Our judges have completed the first cut of half our total contestants, and I have before me, this year's list of ninety-seven pre-liminary finalists from around the globe. When I call your name, please make your way to the front, at which time we will draw for this afternoon's geographic themes. And for those of you who keep track of such things, the names are in no particular order."

The nervous crowd tittered.

"This is it," Beau whispered in Gracie's ear. The heat of his breath gave her chills. "You ready?"

Swallowing hard, she nodded while Ms. Turner began listing names, but truthfully, Gracie wasn't entirely sure how she felt. If she didn't hear her name, she wouldn't die. The world would go on spinning. But if she did…

Hope was still alive. Hope for a wonderful future, including another restaurant all her own and…Beau? Would he be part of her future? Her baby's? Leaning against him, waiting to hear her name called among the dozens of others, she fervently hoped so.

Kalim Obuitz…

Lance Ferguson…

Marcet Foixquette…

Gracie Sherwood...

"*Yes!*" Beau cried out. "I knew it! Congratulations, baby."

"Oh, Gracie!" her mother said with an excited clap. "I'm so proud of you!"

"I knew you could do it, girl," her father said.

The scene was a madhouse of flashbulbs and cheers and soon Caleb, Adam and Gillian were surrounding her, leading Beau and her and her parents away from the boisterous crowd and down a quiet hall.

"What's wrong?" Gracie asked while they practically shoved her into a dull, all-navy-blue conference room. "I worked hard for that moment."

"We know," Caleb said. "And I'm sorry, but in a crowd like that, we can't ensure your safety. Now, we allowed you to compete, but in return, we need you to play by at least a few of our rules."

"Sure," she said, hating the fact that Vicente was here on her special day, even if in the physical sense, he wasn't.

"What's going on?" her father asked. "Why the need for so much added security? I thought Vicente was safely behind bars?"

"He is," Gracie said, using her pleading gaze to implore Caleb to allow her parents to keep their peace of mind.

Caleb looked away from her direct stare, then to her father. "Sir, Vicente escaped from prison twelve days ago. Since that time, several attempts have been made on your daughter's life. While we are able to protect her in a closed setting, we just can't control a mob."

"I understand," her father said, patting Caleb's back. "Thank you for being straight with me."

Lips held in a grim, straight line, Caleb's only answer was a sharp nod.

Gracie's mother looked near tears, but she didn't shed any. Thank God. For if she'd started crying, Gracie worried she'd join in. "Why didn't you tell us sooner?"

Gracie shrugged. "I didn't think it was important."

"Not important?" her mom all but shrieked. Hand clamped over her mouth, she turned away.

"It's all right," Beau said to her parents. "She's got the best security team there is. And now that the first round has ended, hopefully, the crowd will thin out."

"Oh my gosh," Gracie said. "Speaking of the first round being over, I didn't go to the front of the ballroom to draw my afternoon assignment. If I don't show, I'll be disqualified."

"They wouldn't dare," Gillian said, holding up an odd-shaped circle. "After all, you're the future winner."

"You drew for me?" Gracie asked Gillian.

"I did," Adam said. "Hope you don't mind. We prearranged it in the event you were a semifinalist. Figured it would minimize your exposure."

"Thanks…I think." All of the sudden, Gracie didn't feel so hot. The implications of what all of them were doing there hit hard. Apparently they believed Vicente was still out there somewhere, trying to kill her. Even though with Beau, she felt inordinately safe, obviously, all the other marshals assembled felt differently.

"You okay?" Beau asked, leading her to one of eight chairs ringing an oval table.

"Yeah," she said with a wobbly nod. "I think."

"You'd better do more than think," Gillian said, crossing to her to gently knead her shoulders. "You've got another round to win."

Battling a sudden raging bout of nerves over how much was at stake, Gracie asked, "Hey, Adam, what country did *I* draw?"

"Iceland," he said. "But I don't know of anything but pricey vodka and hot blondes that come from there."

God bless Adam who was always good for a laugh.

"Thankfully," Gracie said, "I happen to know of a lot more yummy things from there—although if I weren't lugging this baby around, I could probably use a couple shots of Icelandic vodka."

THE WHOLE of the afternoon, Vicente watched, waited, for a time when the woman he once loved and now despised would be vulnerable. He watched as she prepared her competition dishes. Foods of which he'd once partaken with her. Licked the juices from her fingers.

What was wrong with the woman? What sort of gene was she missing to now be so cold and disloyal? To have apparently forgotten all he'd done for her—

not only personally, but also in her career. What of their vows? Had her promise to love, honor and obey him till death they do part slipped her mind?

In his family, loyalty came above all. But apparently, seeing how words such as loyalty and honor were not among her vocabulary, it was time she learned.

It was time that at death, they did part.

Yes, he'd hired men to help with his marriage's final task, but after seeing her up close and personal that night he'd spirited her from the mountain hotel, he'd released them all from their contracts. This job, he thought, surveying freshly manicured nails, he had to do personally. He had to teach her a lesson in civility. Common courtesy for a husband who'd have given her the world. And what had she given him in return?

Absolutamente nada.

Chapter Thirteen

"I'd like to propose a toast," Joe said that night around the apartment's elegant dining room table, raising a glass of vintage champagne. "To *Kransekake!*"

"To *Kransekake!*" Gracie, Beau, Allie, Joe and Gracie's parents cheered, raising their glasses, as well. Caleb, Adam and Gillian were on duty.

Gracie's Icelandic feast had been a big hit, granting her an invitation to Saturday morning's semifinal round of forty-nine chefs. As she sipped sparkling cider from a lovely champagne flute, Gracie yet again fought the urge to pinch herself to check if the scene was real. How, in less than one week, had she gone from being scared and on her own, to being surrounded by family? And that's what Beau and all her other new friends had become. Suddenly, she had a whole new reason for succeeding. Not just for the seed money to launch her own new restaurant and life for the baby, but also to make these wonderful, generous people proud.

"To Gracie," Joe continued. "May you and your baby girl finally find the peace you deserve."

"Here, here!" Caleb called out, strolling into the room to affectionately rest his hands upon his wife's shoulders. He leaned low to briefly kiss her.

A week earlier, Beau would've found himself jealous of what the two shared, but he now reached for Gracie's hand and squeezed.

"So, Gracie?" Allie called down to the far end of the table. "What're your plans after your big win?"

"I'm going home," she said, still holding his hand.

Upon hearing her decision, her parents beamed, but Beau felt suddenly too warm. Georgia? Even after all they'd shared, she was still going with that plan?

"My parents live in a small town," she said. "If it's okay with you," she directed to her mother, "I'm hoping to bunk with you all until I can maybe get hired as the cook at one of the two local diners or maybe in one of the school cafeterias. I eventually would like to start my own restaurant again, but even if I do have the good fortune to win the competition, finding the right location and menu will take time."

"Well," Allie said, "when you do get set up, I would love to be there opening night."

"Here, here," Joe said again, tipping his near-empty glass. Guess the guy liked champagne. Beau was more a beer or bourbon guy, but hell, judging by the lead weight in his gut, guess he'd have to make do with more of the bubbly stuff. Georgia? Did Gracie have any idea how far that was from everything he loved—that is, aside from her? But then if what he felt for her was truly love, then he'd have to be okay with her decision.

While the rest of the gang nibbled on catered finger foods Allie had ordered through one of the city's best caterers, seeing how Gracie would need to rest up for her next round, Beau clamped his hand over his suddenly throbbing forehead.

"You okay?" Gracie asked in a quiet voice only for him to hear while everyone else gabbed about different celebrity chefs they'd seen at the competition—some even big enough stars that he'd heard of them.

"Sure," he said, giving her a reassuring smile. "Just been a long day."

"Tell me about it." She rested her head on his shoulder, her curls tickling his chin. Having her lean on him for support made him feel strong again. Like a man. Not that he ever wanted her to feel vulnerable without him, just that it was good to feel needed. But couldn't she need him somewhere closer than Georgia?

"Joe," Allie asked, "weren't you saying during that last round how it might be fun to branch into the restaurant biz?"

"Yes, ma'am." Joe finished his champagne and helped himself to more. To Gracie he asked, "What kind of initial investment are we talking to start up your average-size bistro? Although one caveat I'd have is that the establishment be near Portland. Otherwise, what fun is it to own a restaurant if you can't eat there every night to avoid your wife's cooking?" To all assembled, he flashed a teasing wink.

"I heard that!" Gillian hollered from her post in the front hall. "Allie, smack him for me."

"Will do." A playful twinkle in her eyes, Allie abided by her sister-in-law's wishes.

Beau had once hated this part of his family. How they were always horsing around, having such a good time. So now that he was poised to finally be part of all their fun, in that he would soon have a family life all his own to celebrate and be proud of, why was he suddenly so down?

Gee, could it have something to do with the fact that in his heart, he felt committed to Gracie, but apparently, seeing how never once had she mentioned him in her going home speech, she felt none of the same affection?

Adam put his napkin beside his plate. "Don't mean to bust up the party, but I've got to get some zzz's before my next shift."

"Me, too," Caleb said.

"You all are party poopers," Allie complained. To Gracie's parents, she said, "Dixie, Hal, you're not going to abandon me, are you? I was thinking of taking the rest of this kibble to the movie room and vegging out."

"Sounds fun to me," Dixie said.

Hal frowned. "Joe, how about me and you play a few games of pool?"

"I'm with you," Joe said, snatching a few mini egg rolls from a silver patter.

"While you all decide," Gracie said, her voice raspy and tired, "I'm going to bed. Good night everyone. Allie, thanks so much for arranging this party. It was really fun."

"My pleasure, sweetie," Allie said. "Congratulations."

Beau, along with the rest of the men present, stood when Gracie pushed back her chair.

Good nights were made all around with lots more hugging and laughing, before Beau, Gracie leading the way, headed down the hall leading to their rooms.

In front of Gracie's door, he paused, cupping his fingers around her upper arms. "You did great today. I'm proud of you."

"Thanks," she said, gazing up at him with a warm, yet weary smile. She slipped her hands around his waist, resting her cheek on his chest. God, she felt good in his arms. But could he have somehow misread her feelings for him?

"Ready for bed?" she asked.

"Yeah," he said, stepping away from her with a sigh. "Guess so. Well, 'night."

She flashed him a funny, half smile. "Everything okay? You seem strange."

"I'm good," he said with a firm nod. "Just trying to keep up appearances, you know. Don't want to get too close with your folks lurking."

"Sure," she said. "But you'll be in later, right?"

"Yeah."

"Okay, well…" She flopped her hands at her side, then stood on her tip-toes, pressing a soft kiss to his lips that made him instantly hard, instantly wanting nothing more than to spend the night with her nestled sweetly beside him. But after the whole Georgia bit, everything between them had felt…*off*.

He kissed her forehead. "You'd better get some rest. You've got a big day tomorrow."

"I'd sleep better with you," she said.

God, he wanted to go with her, to hold her in his arms all night long. So why didn't he? She'd just handed him an engraved invitation, so why couldn't he follow her through that bedroom door?

Why? Because he was confused as hell, that's why.

Could Caleb be right? Had he rushed this whole thing with Gracie all in some misguided attempt to repair his busted past? Was he playing with fire by not telling her he was officially off the case?

Washing his face with his hands, Beau sighed, then closed Gracie's door—with him on the outside. He had so much to think about, his brain actually hurt.

Hopefully, all he needed was a good night's sleep, then everything would look better in the morning.

"Burkina Faso?" Gracie closed her eyes and tried not to burst into tears. All her studying. Hours and hours of memorizing countries and regional specialties. Yet for all she'd done, after seeing the country she'd drawn for the all-important Saturday morning semifinal round, her mind was a complete blank. Of course, it didn't help that she'd gotten approximately two-and-a-half hours sleep while trying to figure out what she might've said or done to transform Beau from a warmhearted, fun-loving guy to Mr. Freeze.

"It's in Africa if that helps," Beau said, tugging dust covers from her equipment and fresh spices.

She shot him her most evil, slit-eyed stare. "Kinda knew that, but thanks."

"Well? Your blank stare told me you might not. I was only trying to help."

"Contestants, ready!" called a booming voice from the prep area intercom.

"No," Gracie mumbled.

"Begin!"

"What's the plan, boss?"

Think, think...

Gracie pressed her fingers to her temples, but the only thing coming to mind were questions. "Why did you run off last night?"

"Huh?" If possible, he looked more confused than she felt. "Gracie, babe, come on. Focus. Time's a wastin'."

"Trust me," she said. "I know better than anyone

I'm on the clock, but part of my problem is I can't believe how blah you were last night. I mean, we were right in the middle of a party, and you start yawning. At first, my heart started racing," she said, slamming an electric meat grinder she'd taken from the storage area on the stainless steal counter. "You know, I was all giddy inside and thinking, oh boy, we're going to bed—wink, wink. But then *nooooo*, what does my boyfriend do? He seriously wants to sleep! Alone!"

"Whoa—back up. So, you think of me as your boyfriend, but yet during that well-rehearsed speech of yours—remember the one? You outlined your plans for a future in Georgia—without me. Ring any bells?"

"Oh my gosh," she said, grabbing a pack of lamb from their extensive meat stock. "So that's what you were ticked about?" She handed the meat to him. "Grind this."

"I wasn't ticked," he said.

"Then what would you call that slashed eyebrow, tight-lipped expression you wore?"

"Truth? I was sad, all right? Hell, I'm looking forward to meeting your baby. There, I said it, it's out on the table. For as long as I can remember, I've wanted to be a dad, and as much as I love you, I already love your baby."

"But she's not even yours, but the daughter of a psycho criminal."

Slapping the meat pack on the counter, wiping his

hands on his white apron, he went to her, cupping her face in his hands. "Above all, Gracie, she's *your* daughter. Don't you ever forget that. You are a beautiful, precious soul—and so is your baby."

"Stop," she said, instantly crying. "I seriously have to cook."

"Yes, you do," he said, brushing away her tears with the pads of his thumbs, "but first, tell me why I can't come to Georgia with you."

"Why would you want to?" she said. "Your family's here. Your job. I can't ask you to—"

"Did you ever think I wanted to be asked? That maybe you'd be worth the trip?"

"I was afraid," she said. "Both our families are so freaked out by how close we've grown in so little time. Hell—I'm freaked out. I don't know, I thought maybe we should try dating long distance for a while."

"And me miss the miracle of this birth?" He roved his hands down her silhouette to her bulging belly. "I love you. I love her. You're kind of a package deal."

"You don't know what you're saying," she said through sniffles. "It's too soon. Mom says—"

"Hey," he said, lightly tugging her back to the storage area to thoroughly kiss her. "Who're you gonna trust? Your mom—lovely though she is. Or this…" He kissed her again, this time, with a passion that dizzied her, driving away what little remained of her doubts. His amazing kiss inspired her. Energized her. "I don't care how crazy it sounds—*I love you.*"

He kissed her again, smacked her behind, then said, "Now, cook!"

Gracie did cook—like crazy. Forty minutes later, she had five dishes that while she wasn't entirely sure were specifically from Burkina Faso, she was reasonably sure they were at least from that region, which would hopefully be enough to sway judges her way.

The referee called, "Time's up! Chefs, please exit the food presentation areas immediately."

"Whew," Gracie said. "That was tough. Remind me not to waste my first ten minutes gabbing ever again."

"Waste?" he asked, not against taking advantage of the semiprivate storage area to steal a kiss.

"Mmm…" she said. "I stand corrected."

"Damn straight," Beau said. "So? How do you think you did?"

Resting her arms on her belly, she shrugged. "The last two rounds, I felt like *we'd* nailed it. This one…" She shook her head. "I'm not so sure. Only thing I am sure of is that I need to pee—bad."

Laughing, Beau said, "Let me signal Gillian to give you an escort." Since the stage area was closed access, Gillian was posted at one end, Caleb on the other. Adam, Mulgrave and two other agents kept a roving eye on the audience, which because of the bright stage lighting, Gracie and Beau weren't able to see.

At the rear entrance to their stage kitchen, Beau

looked both ways, then led Gracie to the north entrance to where Gillian stood watching guard. "Gil, think you could run the chef to the bathroom?"

"Sure." After mumbling something into the microphone tucked up the sleeve of her dark pantsuit, Gillian scanned the area, then, hand on Gracie's back, led her through the crowd.

From seemingly out of nowhere, Adam, Caleb and Mulgrave appeared, surrounding Gracie in still more dark-suited protection. Beau tagged along, but not as part of the immediate group.

"How'd it go?" Gillian whispered.

"Eh…" Gracie teetered her hand in the universal sign of so-so. "I've felt better about a contest round, but hopefully some of my competition did lousy, too."

"Right," Gillian said with a laugh. "I've sampled enough of your cooking to know nothing you make ever turns out bad. Well…" She grinned. "Except for that weird egg soup Beau told me about."

"Ha ha," Gracie said with a wincing grin of her own. "Sad, but true."

"Hang tight," Gillian said, "while I check out the rest room for criminal types who may or may not resemble your ex-husband."

"Great, but hurry," Gracie urged, trying super hard not to do the pee-pee dance right there in front of the world.

"All clear," Gillian said a few minutes later, leading Gracie inside.

"Thanks." Whew. Gracie headed into a stall, breathing a huge sigh of relief that she'd made it in time.

Finished, she went to the sink, holding her hands under warm water. "Gillian?" Gracie glanced over her shoulder, but Beau's sister wasn't there. Odd, but not unheard of.

Imaging herself back in her bedroom bath's big, wonderful tub, Gracie closed her eyes. What a strange dichotomy of a morning. Though the competition had been a disaster, her talk with Beau had been inspired. It was hard to believe he'd been upset because he'd thought she didn't want him.

Ha! If he'd ever kissed himself, he'd know *not* wanting him was impossible!

She opened her eyes to turn off the faucets and make sense of her hair, but when she peered into the mirror, it wasn't wayward curls claiming her attention, but a gun, held in the steady, outstretched hand of her ex. He wore an outrageous disguise, but even with blond hair, blue eyes and bad teeth, she'd know him anywhere.

"Good afternoon," he said while she struggled for air.

This wasn't happening. No way was he here.

"W-where's Gillian?" Gracie somehow managed to ask.

"Disposed of."

"Y-you killed her?"

With his free hand, he removed a stick of gum from the lapel pocket of an incredibly tacky, blue seersucker suit.

"She'll live—possibly. That is, if you cooperate."

"What'd you to do to her?" Gracie demanded.

"Nothing too permanent—assuming you follow directions."

Swallowing hard, Gracie thought of not Gillian the marshal, but Gillian the mom and wife. Back in Portland, Meggie needed her. And Chrissy, her baby girl. And Joe. Dear, sweet, funny Joe. "A-anything," she said, mind and pulse racing to think of an escape. Hands protectively over her stomach, she said, "I'll do anything you want, just please, let Gillian live."

"Of course, you'll do anything," he said. "Starting with going into that storage closet, then accompanying me out into the service corridor."

"B-but—"

"Gracie? Gil?" It was Caleb shouting through the partially open door. "Everything all right?"

"Answer him," Vicente said, voice barely a whisper, gun pointed between Gillian's eyes where she lay unconscious on the floor of the last stall.

Seconds felt like hours. Gracie knew if she screamed, Vicente would kill Gillian. If she stayed quiet, he'd shoot her. It wasn't a question, but fact.

Unless…If she agreed to go with him, then escaped.

"Grace? Gillian?" Caleb called again.

"We're fine!" Gracie sang out. "Gillian's just taking a turn."

"'Kay. Just checking."

"Good girl," Vicente said, rising, then waving his gun toward the closet.

Gracie darted for the door leading to freedom. To Caleb and the rest of her marshals and most especially, Beau. But she was no match for Vicente, who easily outpaced her, then ground the icy barrel of his gun against her still bruised left temple. "I'd prefer killing you right here," he too calmly said, "but then your friends would storm in here and play the heroes, marching me back to prison like a bad little boy." Chuckling, he shook his head, gripping her roughly by her upper arm, then shoving her into the dimly lit storage closet before closing and locking the door.

Chapter Fourteen

"It's been too long," Beau said when two more minutes had passed and there was still no sign of Gracie or Gillian leaving the rest room. "I'm going in," he said in a matter-of-fact tone to all assembled.

"The hell you are," Caleb said. "You're off the case, remember?"

"Well, since you're on the case, then," he said in his most sarcastic tone, "how about checking if the ladies are okay?"

Caleb shot his younger, cockier brother a look, then proceeded into the ladies' room, expecting to find his sister and Gracie standing at the sink, sharing makeup tips or maternity stories.

What he did find made his blood run cold.

His sister lay unconscious, her body crumpled and prone in the last stall.

He felt for a pulse and thank God, she was still alive. A rag lay to the side of the toilet. Chloroform?

"Get an ambulance!" he shouted into his microphone. "Gillian's down!"

Adam and Beau stormed into the restroom.

"She alive?" Adam asked.

"Yeah. Just out cold."

"And Gracie?" Beau didn't want to ask.

To Adam, Caleb said, "Stay with Gil. Mulgrave, loan loverboy your piece."

"Screw you," Beau said, reaching into his apron to pull out his .38. "I've already got one."

Caleb just shot him a look before trying the storage closet door. When he found it locked, he shot it.

When the smoke cleared, it creaked open.

With no one left guarding the bathroom door, a civilian wandered in and screamed, which only ignited more panic.

"Adam! Mulgrave," Caleb barked, "how 'bout a little crowd control? Beau, follow me!"

They entered the dark closet only to exit through another door.

"Smooth," Beau said. "Why the hell wasn't this checked out before Gracie and Gil walked right into that trap?"

"It was," Caleb said. "Oh, hell…"

Beau looked down the dark service corridor, lit only by eerie red emergency lighting, then retched. His old pal, Wolcheck, lay at an impossible angle that could only mean one thing. He was dead.

Caleb knelt beside him, but no matter how much

seeing a long-time friend twisted like this knifed his gut, he had to keep going. "Come on," he said to his brother. "We can't help him, but maybe, if we're lucky, we can still save Gracie."

Running, running down the endless hall, dodging five gallon drums of cleaning fluids and all manner of vacuums and buffers and ladders, Beau prayed.

Please, God, let her be all right. Please, don't do this to me again. Don't take the woman I love. Don't take another baby I love.

Gracie woke disoriented with an awful taste in her mouth. "Beau?"

Only after she'd spoken his name, did the events of that afternoon come hurtling back. Their argument, their making up. The competition. The reunion with her psycho ex. Was Gillian all right? Beau? Her parents? Caleb and Allie and Joe and the rest of the gang? Why? Why, when she was part of a wonderful family had her shot at happiness been snatched away?

She pushed herself up only to bring her filthy hands to her mouth, staring wide-eyed in horror at cold, stark surroundings that were a far cry from the gracious historic hotel where she'd spent the morning.

Sweating, concrete walls formed the backdrop for a nightmarish scene. On a metal folding chair, seated across from the pile of dirty blue moving blankets she'd been asleep on was Vicente. Legs crossed, dark hair and suit immaculate. Holding an unlit cigar, he could've been the man she'd so long ago married. Only he wasn't. The lack of soul in his black eyes gave him away.

"Good afternoon, my love," he said with a gracious smile. "Have a pleasant rest?"

"What'd you drug me with? Will it hurt my baby?"

He shrugged, meticulously went about the business of lighting his cigar. Even under the best of circumstances, she'd never liked the smell. Now, it brought bile rising to the back of her throat.

"Answer me, damn you." She lunged for him, only to find her arms and legs shackled. She screamed in frustration, but it did little good. She might as well have been screaming at a block of ice. The man wasn't human.

"I talked to *Mamá* this morning. She always had a fondness for you. In fact, she sent her love. Asked me for your number so that she could occasionally call. Check on you for herself." He laughed. Shook his head. "She said you were good for me. I didn't have the heart to tell her she was mistaken."

"What's wrong with you?" Gracie asked on a sob. "What did I ever do to make you hate me to this degree?"

"Ever heard of a thing called loyalty? You freely partook of my hard-won wealth, only to then stab me in the back by turning my private diary over to authorities. Where I come from, family comes before all else."

He took another drag off his cigar, then reached to the foam cooler she'd just now noticed beside him. On top sat a gun with what she'd guess from the few cop shows she'd watched was a silencer. He stroked the weapon using the same motions he'd used in their marital bed. To think she'd once welcomed his touch sickened her.

She squeezed her eyes closed, willing herself from this awful place, back to the enchanted garden where she and Beau had first kissed. No—that was wrong. That moment on the swing hadn't been their first, but second time to touch lips. Their first had been when Beau had saved her from Vicente's last attempt to silence her. Beau had saved her then, and if she didn't save herself, first, she prayed he'd soon save her again.

"Thinking of your boyfriend?" Vicente asked with a putrid smirk.

"Go to hell."

"Such foul language. Tsk, tsk. You must be mindful of what you say. Such things tend to scar newborns."

"Oh—and like whatever you used to knock me out won't?"

He sighed. "Here we go again. Talking in circles. I had such high hopes for us. And now… Look at you. Grossly overweight. Dark circles under your eyes. Clothes ragged and torn. Hair—" He shook his head. "I could go on, but what would be the point? Anyway, very shortly, I will be giving you an injection which will help you permanently sleep. I had first planned to just shoot you, but so messy." He shuddered. "All that blood. Upon your death, it will be a simple matter of putting you aboard my jet, then flying you home to my true family where you will be buried in the family plot."

"You're insane!" she spat. "I was your wife! I'm carrying your baby!"

Yawning, he said, "I've grown so tired of you— not to mention your country's queer manner of justice. Because I find you somewhat amusing, and disposing of a body in broad daylight is not generally wise, I will let you live until sundown, but when that time comes, rest assured, despite our history, despite the baby, you *will* die."

"BEAU," Caleb said, leaning across the dining room table where only last night they'd sat around to casually eat. "Get a grip, man. Vicente's plane is surrounded. We've discovered his assumed name and searched the hotel room he was booked in. You should know better than anyone, when he wants to be, the man's a ghost. I don't know what more we can do."

Gillian, still weak, but okay, tried putting her arm around him, but Beau brushed her away.

He didn't want comfort.

Not now, when God only knew what that bastard of an ex was doing to Beau's beautiful Gracie. And she was his. No matter what anyone said about how improbable it was that the two of them felt what they did, plain and simple, they loved each other.

Beau would die himself before he let that bastard, Vicente, harm her.

Gracie's mother had been so distraught upon hearing the news of her daughter's kidnapping, that under doctor's orders, for her own safety, she'd been tranquilized. Hal, Gracie's father, was in their bedroom with her, staring silently at a wall.

Beau, meanwhile, felt responsible.

If only he'd done as she'd asked and not officially quit her security team. Damn the rules. Their love was bigger than some manual on how he was supposed to have behaved. He adored her. Her baby. Had probably loved them both since that night Gracie had first put his hand on her belly to feel the baby move.

His eyes stung from the agonizing feeling of helplessness settling low in his gut.

"We'll find her," Allie said, kneading his shoulders. "Adam's been on the phone all afternoon with local police."

"Swell," Beau said with a sarcastic snort. "It's been hours since she vanished, and they don't even have any leads. That makes me feel just great."

Shoving back his chair, Beau stood.

"Where are you going?" Caleb asked.

Beau shot them all go-to-hell looks. "To find Gracie myself."

GRACIE WOKE to a fresh nightmare.

Vicente was no longer in the room, but golden, late afternoon sun slanted in a ray of hope from the edge of stained blinds covering two small windows at the basement's far left corner.

She was still chained at both her wrists and ankles, and for a moment, she tried struggling, but it was no use. Unless the cavalry arrived, she'd be going nowhere soon.

BEAU STOOD outside the hotel's service door entrance that it'd been proven by prints Vicente and Gracie had left through.

The air was oppressive. Muggy and hot. It smelled of putrid food waste and exhaust from a delivery truck idling at a loading dock not twenty yards away at the center of one of three buildings behind the hotel.

A crew of Hispanics off-loaded oranges.

Bags and bags of oranges.

In light of Gracie's kidnapping, the next and final round of the competition had been postponed. Despite her misgivings about her latest performance, she had made it to the final round, of which only 12 of a starting field of 193 international chefs would be represented.

Aside from the local cops and additional marshals still scouring the scene for any clues as to where Vicente was temporarily hanging out, the public areas of the hotel had been cleared, guests asked to remain in their rooms until an all-clear had been sounded.

Though Beau's head spun, his heart raced and mouth was dry, he clamped his palms over his eyes, willing thoughts to come. What was he missing? What did he know about all of this that the average guy on the case wouldn't?

Obviously, like the night Vicente had first taken Grace, he was a ghost, blending with the scenery, or like on hotel surveillance tapes, Vicente also had a knack for hiding in plain view.

That said, what would be his next move?

Obviously, if the guy wanted to make it out of San Francisco, he didn't dare draw attention to himself. There'd been no dramatic, squalling-tire car seen tearing down city streets.

"*Más rápidamente!*" the apparent leader of the loading crew shouted, darting a look over his shoulder, then down the alley toward two uniformed cops. "*Haga apenas bastante sitio para el cargo nuevo!*"

Beau looked toward the hustling crew, resentful that in the midst of the biggest tragedy he'd ever suffered, life would go on. How dare these men act as if everything was normal when—

Parts of his brain fired that hadn't been used since high school. *El cargo nuevo? New cargo.*

But if those guys were dropping off a load of fruit, then why would they—

Already running in that direction, Beau called the safe house for back up.

Every nerve in his body told him Vicente the ghost was close—very close. For what better way to perform the perfect escape then to never have left?

GRACIE'S HEAD spun while she struggled to stay awake. Vicente had obviously drugged her again. But with what? And what would it do to her precious baby girl?

Heavy footfalls floated to her from across the cavernous space. The sunbeams were longer now, almost gone, save for a thin stream decorated with incongruously happy dust motes.

From the footsteps floated a voice. "I'm so sorry to be the bearer of bad news," Vicente said, smoothly gliding her way. "But your driver is early. I told him we wouldn't be finished with our business until after dark, but he assures me his men can invisibly get you to my plane. Oh—and this may be of interest to you…" He took a cigar from his coat pocket, clipped off the end before taking his time about lighting it. In her daze, the flame looked ethereal. Beautiful in a strangely sinister way. "In case you harbored thoughts of rescue, your silly marshals have surrounded my plane—only it's the wrong one. How stupid do they think I am?" Tsk-tsking, he shook his head.

"Please, let me go," she said, hating the fact that she'd been reduced to begging, but hating worse the thought of dying without ever meeting her baby. Or, ever again seeing Beau. Dear, sweet Beau.

"Oh, I will," he said, strolling toward her pile of filthy blankets. Kneeling beside her, cloying cigar smoke making her nostrils flair and stomach retch, he ran the backs of his fingers along her still faintly bruised cheek, crawling them down her jaw.

A scream formed low in her throat, only no matter how hard she tried, her voice felt incapable of sound. Obviously he'd drugged her again. Or maybe these were lingering effects from last time.

Was her baby all right? If only she'd move. Give Gracie some desperately needed sign she wasn't alone.

"You're trembling," Vicente said. "Excited, are you? It has been awhile since we've last touched. You've no doubt missed me."

When she said nothing, he quietly laughed. "No need to fear, my pet, in death, you shall have time aplenty to remember the pleasure you threw away."

Moaning, struggling with her chains, Gracie wished she was the fainting type, because she really, truly didn't want to be awake when she died.

Gracie couldn't stop shaking as her monster of an ex ground out his cigar on the concrete floor only to begin stroking his gun.

She was too panicked to breathe, and desperately tried to recall happier times. Times with Beau when her life had been so close to achieving that much sought after, blissful state called *normal.*

Standing, aiming the gun at her head, Vicente pulled the trigger.

Upon hearing the soft swoosh of the silenced bullet leaving the chamber, she flinched, only to silently sob upon realizing he must've aimed over her head.

"Oops," he said with another of his sickeningly calm smiles. "I'd better be careful. Wouldn't want to draw blood when here I've already decided poisoning you would be a cleaner, more efficient way to go."

From some primal instinct to save her baby, to stay alive, Gracie found her scream, then wildly tugged at the cuffs and chains binding her in place.

"Oh, that will never do," Vicente said. "I had planned on keeping this civilized, but you've left me no choice but to gag you." From his lapel pocket, he pulled a black satin scarf. "Open wide," he said, holding it over her mouth.

Thrashing her head from side to side, she screamed for all she was worth.

"Damn you," he said, for the first time showing emotion. Dropping the scarf in favor of holding the gun to her bulging stomach, he said, "You must stay still and quiet, or I promise to make this a thousand times harder."

"No!" she cried. "Please. I'll do anything! I won't testify! Just please don't hurt my baby!"

Crash!

The sound of broken glass came as music to Gracie's ears.

"The only one getting hurt around here, Delgado, is you! Put down the gun!" Gracie couldn't be sure she wasn't hallucinating, but either way, Beau was in the window, punching out the blind, then aiming his gun at Vicente's head.

Vicente just laughed, firing off two rounds at Beau, then hurtling himself behind a metal storage locker.

Beau again fired, but metal pinging against metal told her his intended target had been missed. And then her beloved was shimmying through the window, his hands bloodied from broken glass.

"Beau, no!" Gracie cried. "Don't come any closer!"

Too late.

A shot was fired, and then Beau was hopping around, swearing as blood pulsed from his calf. "The bastard shot me!"

Hopping to the other side of the massive space, taking shelter behind an abandoned industrial washer, Beau fired two more shots, but again hit only metal.

"Stupid man," said Vicente, creeping up behind him. "What's it going to take for you to die?"

"No!" Gracie screamed. "Please, Vicente! If you ever loved me, *please* don't hurt him. It's me you want. I'm the one who ruined your good name. But I promise not to testify. I'll even help you get away."

"Stop it, Gracie," Beau said, fighting to clear his swimming head. "Y-you're trying to reason with a psychopath." Dammit, how could he have been so careless as to get shot?

"Please, Vicente. Forgive me. I'm so sorry for being disloyal. I was wrong."

Beau had a hard time finding his next breath.

He looked down.

The concrete at his feet was pooled with blood. In his periphery vision, the already gray day faded to black, and then Beau went down.

"Gracie! Beau!" Adam exploded through double doors leading to Gracie and his brother's tomb.

His frenetic gaze first landed on a pasty-white Gracie and the sick son of a bitch standing over her pregnant belly with a gun.

Not thinking, just doing, Adam shot Vicente Delgado between his beady, black eyes.

"HEY," Beau said to Gracie a day later, hardly able to speak past the hard knot of tears welling the back of his throat. Lying in the hospital bed, hooked up to a zillion machines, she looked small and pale, but alive.

Mirroring a steady beep, a monitor on the window side of the bed printed proof of her baby's strong heart.

"Hey, yourself," she said, casting him that dear smile he wouldn't have lived through another day without. "Hear that?"

He nodded, tucking his crutches under his arms so he could hold out his hand. "May I?" He gestured to the baby, currently doing visible back flips inside her bulging belly.

Tears pooling in her big blue eyes, she nodded, taking her hand in his, leading him to the action. "I think she's got her days mixed up and she thinks it's still Saturday night. Time to party. Only what she doesn't know is that the party's over—at least for me." She looked down, fumbled her hands at her waist. Upon doctors' orders that she was to be on complete bedrest for the next several days, she'd withdrawn from the competition. The CAI executive committee voted unanimously to grant her a bye to the final round for next year.

"Stop," Beau said. "I probably should've mentioned this earlier, but in case you didn't know, you're about to have a baby. When you won, now wouldn't have been the greatest time to start a press tour, anyway."

Knowing he was right didn't make the reality of her situation any easier. "Trouble is," she said, "I had all these plans. Starting over again, you know."

"Yeah, I know," he said, covering her hands where she'd splayed them over her belly. He interlocked their fingers, loving the feel of her. The soft, soapy smell. "But, look, I know you were going to go back to Georgia with your folks, but this close to your due date, I've been thinking, how about you just stay with me? I've got a big, old rambling wreck of a house that's not pretty but has plenty of room. We'll make a party of it, Dixie and Hal can stay, too."

"You lied to me," she said. "Why?"

"Huh?" Here he was in a roundabout way proposing and she wanted to discuss ancient history?

"You know, about you having quit the marshal's service."

"I didn't quit," he said. "Just took a vacation."

"Why didn't you tell me? Why did you let me go on believing you were still officially on my case?"

Gazing out the window, at the rain-streaked day, he shrugged. "I didn't figure it mattered."

She struggled with a laugh. "I just escaped my psycho ex who just happened to lie to me about every aspect of our life, yet you didn't think honesty with my current partner mattered?"

"I'm sorry. What more do you want me to say?"

Turning away from him, taking her hands back to wipe silent tears, she said quietly, "I want you to again promise me you'll never lie—and this time, I want you to mean it."

"O-okay."

"I'm serious, Beau. I love you, but not enough to put up with anything other than full-on truth."

"Fair enough. I'm sorry."

"Apology accepted."

"Then you'll marry me?"

Eyebrows raised, she asked, "I wasn't aware the question was even on the table."

"Well, what'd you think I meant when I asked you to move in with me?"

Hand to her forehead, she said, "I'm thinking we've got the kissing and making love part of our relationship down pat, but we might need to work on communication."

"Agreed," he said. "Think in seventy or so years we might figure each other out?"

"It'll be a start."

"Cool. Then it's a deal?"

"What?"

"Woman…" Shaking his head, laughing, he said, "Sometimes I gotta wonder if we're even on the same planet. What do you think we've been talking about? Before you have the baby, I'd like for her to have my name." Squeezing Gracie's hands, he said, "I'd like you to have my name."

"Beau—that's incredibly sweet, but you don't have to—"

"Oh, I know I don't *have* to. I want to. Otherwise, how else am I going to be sure I won't wake one morning with the two of you taking off on a road trip of your own?" He smiled, but she saw by the fear in his eyes that he truly did worry she might up and leave him again.

"I would rather marry you than win fifteen Culinary Olympics."

"That's good," he said. "'Cause in case you hadn't heard, you kind of lost."

"Gee, thanks," she said, landing a halfhearted swat to his sleeve.

"Sure. But on the flip side. In light of recent events, your story made the front page of nearly every paper in the country. And according to Gillian, who's appointed herself your manager, she's been fielding quite a few *hot* offers for you to not just enter more competitions, but be the head chef at restaurants around the country. Which is just one more reason why I'd like to go ahead and pin you down."

"*Pin me down?* Is that your idea of a romance?"

He made a face. "Guess that was every bit as lame as my last stab at a proposal?"

She nodded. "Lucky for you, I'm stuck here for at least the next few days, or so. Hopefully by then, you can come up with something better."

"How about this?" he asked, taking her ring finger, then plucking from the chest pocket of his navy T-shirt the most gorgeous diamond solitaire she'd ever seen. "Gracie Sherwood, I love you. Please, please be my wife. And don't *ever* leave me again. There? Did that work?"

"Mmm…" she said with a grin of utter contentment as he slipped the ring on her finger. "That'll do just fine."

Epilogue

Two Years Later

Joe raised his glass. "To Chef Gracie—Portland's *Chef of the Year* and the best lobster bisque cooker this side of the Rockies."

"Here, here!" Caleb said.

Gracie's husband piped in with, "What about *Best Kisser?*"

"Beau!" Gracie said, reddening as she gave him a swat. "Behave. There are children present—not to mention my parents."

He rolled his eyes. "There are *always* rugrats present. And since your folks moved out here, seems like they're around a lot, too. Anyway," he said with a rogue's wink, "hasn't stopped me yet." And to prove it, he laid one on her right there in front of the whole family. She'd have swatted him again, but his kisses were just too darned good.

"*Mom-ma?*" Katherine—Katy, for short, named

in honor of Gracie's favorite great-aunt who'd died at a ripe old age in her sleep, three years previously—tugged on Gracie's dress sleeve.

"What, sweetie?" Gracie asked.

"Cal *tuk Bar-bee.*"

Ten-year-old Cal piped in with, "She took my GI Joe boat first."

Beau rolled his eyes, then scooped Katy onto his lap. "I'd say this is a job for Judge Allie."

"Hey, leave me out of it," Allie protested. "I'm on maternity leave. Cal, just give her back her doll."

"Not until she gives me my boat—and wipes off the pink nail polish."

As the debate raged on, Gracie gazed at the loving chaos of her wonderful new family. In some wondrous turn of fate, this had become her norm. Raucous Sunday dinners around the family table at *Chez Bon*— the new restaurant she'd started with Gillian and Joe. The place, like the family, was a labor of love.

Most days, far from *Normalville,* but smack dab in the middle of *Perfectville.* And she wouldn't have it any other way.

* * * * *

Watch for the next book in
Laura Marie Altom's U.S. MARSHALS *series,*
TO CATCH A HUSBAND
Coming July 2006, only from
Harlequin American Romance.

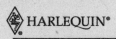

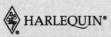

With these women, being single never means being alone

Lauren, a divorced empty nester, has tricked her editor into thinking she is a twentysomething girl living the single life. As research for her successful column, she hits the bars, bistros, concerts and lingerie shops with her close friends. When her job requires her to make a live television appearance, can she keep her true identity a secret?

The Single Life
by Liz Wood

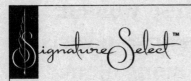

You're never too old to sneak out at night

BJ thinks her younger sister, Iris, needs a love interest. So she does what any mature woman would do and organizes an Over-Fifty Singles Night. When her matchmaking backfires it turns out to be the best thing either of them could have hoped for.

Over 50's Singles Night

by Ellyn Bache

If you enjoyed what you just read,
then we've got an offer you can't resist!

Take 2 bestselling love stories FREE!

Plus get a FREE surprise gift!

Clip this page and mail it to Harlequin Reader Service®

IN U.S.A.	**IN CANADA**
3010 Walden Ave.	P.O. Box 609
P.O. Box 1867	Fort Erie, Ontario
Buffalo, N.Y. 14240-1867	L2A 5X3

YES! Please send me 2 free Harlequin American Romance® novels and my free surprise gift. After receiving them, if I don't wish to receive anymore, I can return the shipping statement marked cancel. If I don't cancel, I will receive 4 brand-new novels every month, before they're available in stores! In the U.S.A., bill me at the bargain price of $4.24 plus 25¢ shipping & handling per book and applicable sales tax, if any*. In Canada, bill me at the bargain price of $4.99 plus 25¢ shipping & handling per book and applicable taxes**. That's the complete price and a savings of at least 10% off the cover prices—what a great deal! I understand that accepting the 2 free books and gift places me under no obligation ever to buy any books. I can always return a shipment and cancel at any time. Even if I never buy another book from Harlequin, the 2 free books and gift are mine to keep forever.

154 HDN DZ7S
354 HDN DZ7T

Name _____ (PLEASE PRINT)

Address _____ Apt.# _____

City _____ State/Prov. _____ Zip/Postal Code _____

Not valid to current Harlequin American Romance® subscribers.

Want to try two free books from another series?
Call 1-800-873-8635 or visit www.morefreebooks.com.

* Terms and prices subject to change without notice. Sales tax applicable in N.Y.
** Canadian residents will be charged applicable provincial taxes and GST.
All orders subject to approval. Offer limited to one per household.
® are registered trademarks owned and used by the trademark owner and or its licensee.

AMER04R   ©2004 Harlequin Enterprises Limited

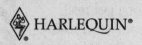

HARLEQUIN®

American ROMANCE®

COMING NEXT MONTH

#1113 MASON'S MARRIAGE by Tina Leonard
Cowboys by the Dozen
When the sheriff from Malfunction Junction discovers he's a father, he's delighted, even if the news comes four years late. Naturally, Mason assumes he'll finally have the only two women he's ever wanted. But Mimi Cannady expects to be wooed, and for a lifelong bachelor that's a tall order—like being asked to do the two-step with two left feet.

#1114 ONE DADDY TOO MANY by Debra Salonen
Sisters of the Silver Dollar
Kate's ex-husband wants joint custody of their daughter, but Kate can't forgive his betrayal. She hires lawyer Rob Brighten to fight the case and finds herself falling in love. But little Maya only wants her "real" daddy. Now, what's a good mother to do?

#1115 TEXAS BORN by Ann DeFee
Olivia Alvarado, vet and local coroner in Port Serenity, Texas, can't stay away from sexy sheriff C. J. Baker, even though she wants to. (Or does she?) She and C.J. are professionally connected by murder—and by mutts (once C.J. gets a dog). And if he has his way, they'll be *personally* connected, too. By marriage...

#1116 CAPTURING THE COP by Michele Dunaway
In the Family
Thirty years of good behavior was enough for anyone, even perpetual virgin Olivia Johnson, minister's daughter. And that was an understatement! Fortunately, it took just a glance at handsome detective Garrett Krause for her to get a few good ideas about some bad behavior—and how to make up for lost time.

www.eHarlequin.com

HARCNM0406